"Well, it's well past quitting time," Shayla pointed out. "Time for all good little detectives to call it a night and go home." She looked at her partner. "We could get started reading those reports first thing in the morning."

"We could," he agreed.

That did *not* sound convincing to her. "Why do I think that you plan to be up all night reading?" she asked.

He didn't bother confirming or denying her supposition. Instead, he said, "Because you're probably the most opinionated woman I've ever crossed paths with."

Rather than take offense, Shayla pretended he had meant it as a joke. "Flatterer."

Gabriel opened his mouth to say something, then closed it again, shaking his head. "It wasn't meant to be flattering."

Shayla's mouth curved. "I always try to make the best of a situation. Are you really determined to read through those reports you have?"

He knew he could just dismiss her assumption, but he also knew that she wouldn't believe him. Those blue eyes of hers just seemed to have a way of looking straight into a man'

The idea both intr

uncomfortable.

Dear Reader,

Welcome back to the world of the Cavanaughs. Shayla Cavanaugh (O'Bannon) is the baby of her branch of the family. She has just recently passed her detectives' exam and her new career begins with a bang. Specifically, a serial killer has unexpectedly changed his hunting grounds from Los Angeles to Shayla's hometown of Aurora. As it turns out, Shayla's new partner is a recent transfer from Los Angeles himself and the Moonlight Killer, as the killer has been dubbed by the press, has followed him. Taunting Detective Gabriel Cortland is a perk the serial killer cannot do without. To that end, before moving on from Los Angeles, the Moonlight Killer added Detective Cortland's wife to his tally, something that almost drove Cortland over the edge—until his determination to avenge his wife's murder brought him back and gave him a reason to live.

Shayla sees the torment in her new partner's eyes, and she is determined not just to help him track down the Moonlight Killer but also to help bring Cortland back among the living. He, of course, views her as meddlesome and interfering, but then, he has a lot to learn about both the Cavanaugh men and the Cavanaugh women. Come watch his education begin.

I hope you enjoy this newest saga about the Cavanaughs, and I hope that in writing it, I have managed in some small way to entertain you. Thank you, as always, for buying one of my books, and from the bottom of my heart, I wish you someone to love who loves you back.

Love,

Marie Ferrarella

CAVANAUGH JUSTICE: DEADLY CHASE

Marie Ferrarella

HARLEQUIN®
ROMANTIC SUSPENSE™

Recycling programs
for this product may
not exist in your area.

ISBN-13: 978-1-335-75974-0

Cavanaugh Justice: Deadly Chase

Harlequin Enterprises ULC
22 Adelaide St. West, 41st Floor
Toronto, Ontario M5H 4E3, Canada
www.Harlequin.com

Printed in U.S.A.

USA TODAY bestselling and RITA® Award–winning author **Marie Ferrarella** has written over three hundred books for Harlequin, some under the name Marie Nicole. Her romances are beloved by fans worldwide. Visit her website, marieferrarella.com.

Books by Marie Ferrarella

Harlequin Romantic Suspense

Cavanaugh Justice

Cavanaugh's Bodyguard
Cavanaugh Fortune
How to Seduce a Cavanaugh
Cavanaugh or Death
Cavanaugh Cold Case
Cavanaugh in the Rough
Cavanaugh on Call
Cavanaugh Encounter
Cavanaugh Vanguard
Cavanaugh Cowboy
Cavanaugh's Missing Person
Cavanaugh Stakeout
Cavanaugh in Plain Sight
Cavanaugh Justice: The Baby Trail
Cavanaugh Justice: Serial Affair
Cavanaugh Justice: Deadly Chase

The Coltons of Colorado

Colton's Pursuit of Justice

Visit the Author Profile page at Harlequin.com for more titles.

To Mama,

Who Gave Me

My First Agatha Christie Book

And Began My

Never-Ending

Love Affair With Murder Mysteries.

I Miss You, Mama,

More Than Words Can Ever Say—

Even Mine

Prologue

It was back.

That itch, that need, that unshakable, overwhelming desire that always began small—sometimes no bigger than a tiny pinprick.

Hardly noticeable at all, he thought with a self-satisfied smile.

But that desire would continue to grow, consuming him until it was all he could think about. Morning, noon and night, it became his constant companion, demanding attention, demanding satisfaction, until that itch, that desire to watch a beautiful face begin to fade as the light slowly went out of that woman's eyes, was all there was.

A light that was extinguished because *he* had been the one to put it out.

Well, technically, he corrected himself, the women

were the ones who put that light out, because eventually when they were able to move again, they began to struggle. And when they did, they weren't able to keep their legs up in a position that didn't cause the thin rope he had artfully tied them up with to be pulled.

When that happened, they would wind up strangling themselves, no matter how hard they tried not to.

In some cases, it was a slow, drawn-out process accompanied by tears when the women he had chosen for this demise realized that there was no way out.

Usually, however, the end process was quick, because the woman who thrashed about thought if she moved with enough force, she could break the string.

The string never broke.

The last time around had wound up being so fast, he barely had enough time to make himself comfortable as he began to watch the young woman squirming about.

He felt cheated, like a boxing patron who had paid the high price of a ticket to watch an exclusive match only to have the match over in a matter of moments due to a well-placed knockout punch.

It had barely satisfied his need to exercise dominance over this holier-than-thou woman who enjoyed looking down her nose at him, acting as if he was less than the lint that accumulated on her clothing because of a faulty dryer.

Not one of these women whom he had ended had the brains of a canary, while he was the superior being, the one with not one science degree, but several. He was the one who could not only dispense the medication that some third-rate physician prescribed, but he actually knew how to mix the different ingredients together to create those medications if necessary.

The women who became his victims thought that because they were lucky enough, through no effort of their own, to have been gifted with great faces and fantastic bodies, that made them his superior. That gave them the right to look right past him as if he didn't even exist.

They changed their minds quickly enough in their final hours, he thought with an almost gleeful smile.

After a moment, the smile turned dark.

They deserved what he did to them. Each and every one of them deserved to be on the receiving end of his wrath.

Except for one.

That had been a truly personal act, even though the woman had no idea who he was.

But her husband did.

What he had done was a warning to the man to get him to back off, that he was getting too close, although, now that he thought about it, the cat-and-mouse game between them did invigorate him.

Too bad the messenger had to be sacrificed, but that was the way it went sometimes.

Besides, he hadn't gotten anything out of that particular kill. Killing that woman hadn't satisfied the fire in his belly. If anything, it just made it grow larger.

He needed to feed that hunger.

Because he had a superior intellect, he knew when things were threatening to close in on him. So he had changed his hunting grounds.

He chuckled to himself. Just when those morons on

the police force thought he was in one place, he had moved his location to another part of Southern California. It would take them weeks to make the connection.

Maybe longer.

Those simpletons never communicated with one another, he thought in satisfaction. Even in this high-tech world, so many things didn't register or wound up falling through the cracks, and those morons on the police force just went stumbling off into the dark.

All except for one.

And now, it seemed that Cortland was back in the game.

And he was ready to play, he thought. Oh, so ready.

He felt the hunger in the pit of his stomach growing.

It had nothing to do with food.

It was time to leave the confines of his new quarters and start patrolling the streets, looking for the next woman who needed to be made to pay.

It was time to play the game again.

He couldn't wait.

Chapter 1

Shayla Cavanaugh-O'Bannon, the youngest of Maeve Cavanaugh-O'Bannon's five children, was admittedly also the sunniest of that subgroup that comprised the many, *many* members of the Cavanaugh clan, most of whom worked in some capacity for the ever-expanding Aurora police department.

Having recently aced her detective's exam, the sharp, pretty, blue-eyed blonde was still learning her way around now that she was an active member of the homicide division and not just part of the uniformed police force.

From the first moment that she had joined up, Shayla had loved everything about being a law enforcement officer. She saw it as a way of being able to help people. Maeve's youngest always focused on the positive aspects of every situation, no matter how dark that situation might seem at the outset.

Determined to make the best impression she could in her new position—there were those who felt that she had only gotten to where she was because of whom her uncle and the rest of her family were and not because of her own merit—Shayla had come in early, which meant that she had gone for her customary run almost in the dark. Invigorated, she'd gotten ready and was at her desk, completing some paperwork.

Paperwork was regarded as the bane of every living law enforcement agent's existence.

She had just decided to get some coffee to help fully focus her brain when she looked up and saw a dark-haired, exceedingly handsome and moody-looking well-dressed man walk by. She was vaguely aware that a new detective had transferred from Los Angeles, although she hadn't met him yet.

His eyes flickered over her for the briefest of moments, but if her presence had registered—Shayla offered him a bright, wide smile—he gave no indication of it. The newcomer just continued walking.

Coffee mug in hand, the twenty-eight-year-old newly minted detective turned and watched the unsmiling man's progress as he walked out the squad room's door and down the hall and then disappeared.

Shayla had always been a sponge when it came to information, whether it was just harmless office gossip or key information that could very well be crucial when it came to solving a case, Shayla took everything in. Which was why, after a moment's pause, she turned toward her older brother Ronan, who just happen to be standing next to her at the coffee machine, and asked, "Is that him?"

The question, coming out of the blue the way it did, caught Ronan completely off guard. Lost in his own thoughts, he had been busy trying to come up with an anniversary gift for his wife, Sierra. He blinked and looked at his sister, whom everyone in the family still thought of as the baby of the group.

"Him who?" Ronan asked. Looking around, he didn't see anyone out of the ordinary in the room—just the same faces he was accustomed to seeing on a more or less daily basis.

"The new guy," Shayla answered, turning back to face her brother, since the person she was asking about had just left the squad room.

She assumed that the new detective was most likely on his way to see the chief of detectives, Brian Cavanaugh.

"Gabriel Cortland—the detective who just transferred here from LA," she elaborated when her brother just continued to look at her, apparently waiting for more input before answering. "What do you know about him?" Shayla asked.

Ronan absently shrugged his broad shoulders. "Only that Cortland was the one who requested the transfer from his old precinct. Word has it he was a really sharp, first-class detective before he fell into the bottle. Almost drank himself to death, but then one day he just decided to get his act together and sober up. And when he did, he put in for a transfer.

"Oh, yeah, and one more thing," her brother added as an after thought. But then he paused, his voice lingering.

Sometimes, getting information out of her brothers was like attempting to drill for water in a well that gave all the appearances of having gone dry, Shayla thought. But she refused to let Ronan see her get frustrated.

"Oh?" she prodded. "And just what is that one thing?"

"Cortland doesn't talk much. Or, from what I hear, practically at all," Ronan told her, draining the last of the coffee from his large mug.

He had a feeling if he didn't leave right now, his sister would just continue asking him questions.

Shayla looked down the hall, despite the fact that the person she was asking about was long gone at this point.

"In other words," she murmured, "a challenge."

"No," her brother told her, "in other words, I'd suggest leaving the man alone. Detective Cortland doesn't strike me as someone who would be a happy recipient of your endless sunshine. They haven't made the kind of sunglasses that can block what you give off."

That didn't begin to convince her that she should back off, not that Ronan had thought that it would. He viewed his youngest sister the same way everyone else in the family did—Shayla was bright and cheery and the absolute definition of unyielding stubbornness once she set her mind on something.

The next words out of Shayla's mouth proved it. "That just tells me that the poor man needs to be subjected to that sunshine, as you put it, even more."

About to leave, Ronan paused and gave her a weary look. "Don't you *ever* come off that cloud of yours?"

"No. Why should I? I don't view the world as a dark, hopeless place," she said in all sincerity.

Ronan almost laughed at her reply. What stopped him was that he believed she honestly meant what she said, which was incredible, yet in a way, he had to admit, also kind of heartwarming.

"Given what you do for a living—what we *all* do," he amended, "that's rather amazing. You are definitely one of a kind, Shayla."

"I really would like to change that," she told her brother with feeling.

"I'm sure you would," he answered. "I've got to go, Shayla. If I do hear anything more about Cortland, I'll pass it on to you," he promised just before he disappeared down the same hallway that the other detective had taken.

Except that unlike the detective under discussion, Ronan was only on his way to the elevator.

Shayla sat at her newly assigned desk—there hadn't been a place for her when she had initially been placed in Homicide until almost a month had gone by.

She remained at her desk for another half hour. At that point, she had finished filling out the paperwork—which wasn't due until tomorrow, at least not by anyone's standards except for her own. Thanks to the work ethic that her mother had instilled in her when she was a little girl, Shayla didn't believe in being on time. She believed in being early—always. To her way of thinking, being early left her time to tackle other things if they came up unexpectedly.

Right now, she was having trouble focusing her attention on anything other than the incredibly sad look in the newly transferred detective's eyes. Try as she might, Shayla couldn't remember ever seeing sadness to that degree.

Oh, to be sure, she had definitely seen sadness before. There was no way she could have been part of the police force without having come in contact with people who had been touched by the ravages of sadness to a lesser or greater degree.

Shayla could remember that look in her mother's eyes when she had received word that their father, a police officer, had been killed in the line of duty.

Eventually, that sadness had faded to some degree.

But the look in Gabriel Cortland's eyes seemed as if it was deeply embedded and very possibly to remain there indefinitely. It wasn't anything that the detective had said—they hadn't exchanged any words—it was just a feeling she'd had during that briefest of moments when their eyes had met in passing.

Still, she *knew* that man was sad. She would bet anything on it. Somehow, some way, she was going to make it her mission to find out what had caused that look, that sadness, to take root. Because if she didn't know what was behind it, she wouldn't be able to help him get beyond it.

And she was determined to do that. For her, it was like walking by a puppy in pain. There was no way she could ignore that puppy. It was no more in her to do that than it was to ignore a cry for help—even a silent one.

Shayla made up her mind. Detective Gabriel Cortland was going to get her help whether he wanted it or not.

Because, at bottom, she was certain that the former LA detective really wanted that help.

Fifteen minutes later found Shayla summoning her courage and going to her uncle's office.

There was a time when her uncle Andrew had been the chief of police, but then his wife had suddenly gone missing, leaving him with five children to raise. Andrew Cavanaugh never thought twice about his course of action. He retired early from the Aurora police force and devoted himself to raising his children, as well as conducting a search for his wife whenever time permitted.

However his younger brother Brian never had to make that sort of life-altering decision, and eventually his dedication got him placed as Aurora's chief of detectives. A levelheaded man who always kept his priorities straight, Brian Cavanaugh never allowed his position to go to his head.

By everyone's account, Chief Brian Cavanaugh was one of the fairest, as well as the most honest, chiefs of detectives the Aurora police department had ever had. He treated everyone the same, taking their merit, not their last name, into account.

The entire family, Shayla thought as she stood in front of the outer door, was exceptionally proud of the work Brian Cavanaugh had done, proud of the man's instincts that always had him running the most efficient police department in the entire state.

He had done all this while raising a combined family of eight—four of his own children, as well as the four offspring that Lila, his former partner, brought into the union when he married her years after his first wife passed away.

Shayla stood there staring at the door that led into her uncle's office, trying to come up with the right words to say, when suddenly she saw a hand reaching up around her and then knocking on that door.

Startled, she swung around and found herself looking up at her uncle.

"The door usually doesn't open unless you knock on it," Brian informed her with a cheerful smile. Opening the door all the way, he glanced down at Shayla. "Would you like to come in?" he asked, even though it was a foregone conclusion.

"Yes, sir," she answered quietly.

The chief of detectives gestured into his office. "Then do that," he coaxed.

Shayla noticed that the desk where her uncle's secretary usually sat, making sure that no one entered the inner sanctum without her say-so, was empty.

Once the newest member of his family to become a detective was in his office, Brian gestured for her to take a chair on the other side of his desk. "And what can I do for you, Detective Cavanaugh?" he asked, his mouth curving ever so slightly as he addressed her formally.

The right words still hadn't come to her. "I'm not sure how to start this, Chief," Shayla admitted nervously.

"The beginning is always a good place to start. That way, you won't lose me," the chief of detectives told her with a wink.

She sincerely doubted that anyone could possibly come remotely close to losing the chief. He was one of the smartest men she knew.

"I might be out of line, sir," Shayla began slowly.

"I'll let you know if you are," he promised in such a friendly tone, they might have been discussing their reaction to one of Andrew Cavanaugh's new dishes, which the family patriarch enjoyed trying out on the family during his far-from-rare get-togethers. It was a well-known fact that the older man used any excuse to throw a party.

Okay. It's now or never, Shayla thought. "Was that the new transfer here to see you earlier? The detective who just transferred from the Los Angeles Police Department," she added in case the chief didn't know whom she was referring to.

"Are you asking about Detective Gabriel Cortland?" her uncle asked.

"Yes, I am," Shayla answered a bit nervously. "Detective Gabriel Cortland," she repeated. "You saw him earlier, right?"

"I did. Shayla." Given the nature of the conversation and her obvious discomfort—an unusual state for her—Brian decided that perhaps it would be better to address the young detective by her first name. "What is this all about?"

"I was wondering, have you assigned him to a partner yet?" she asked, her words pouring out quickly.

"No, I haven't," he replied.

During their meeting, Cortland had specifically said that he wasn't looking to be partnered with anyone. What he was looking for was to be assigned to a specific kind of case. He had said he was rather confident that the serial killer who had been haunting the streets of LA was about to change his hunting grounds.

Brian looked at her with interest. "Why do you ask?"

"Well, if you haven't already assigned him to a partner, I would like to respectfully request that I be the one partnered with Detective Cortland," Shayla told the chief.

To her credit, she thought, she didn't fidget, and she made sure to look him directly in the eye.

Brian nodded his head slowly. "Interesting. May I ask why you're making this request?"

Shayla was confident that the chief of detectives didn't view her as an airhead, or think she was making this request because Gabriel Cortland was an incredibly handsome man by anyone's standards.

She also knew that Brian Cavanaugh wasn't going to laugh at her once she explained. Along with the rest of the family, she and the chief had shared more than a few meals together. Enough meals, she thought, for the chief to believe that she was being serious when she told him why she was making this request.

Still, it took her a moment to try to get her wording just right.

"Because I think he needs me."

Brian looked at her mildly surprised. "Detective Cortland didn't say anything about you," the chief replied, trying to understand just where his niece was going with this.

"That's because he doesn't know who I am," she told him, then realized how she had to sound. "Chief, that man has the saddest eyes I have ever seen. Someone or something hurt Detective Cortland. Hurt him very badly beyond all reason. He needs help in finding his way back among the living." She took a breath. "I know you probably think that I'm crazy—"

"No," he assured her. "I'm intrigued. Continue."

"Those were the eyes of someone who doesn't care if he lives or dies," she told him. "Consequently, he will wind up forging ahead without any hesitation, taking chances the rest of us wouldn't. I would like to be partnered with Cortland so I can watch over him. Possibly convince him that no matter what happened, he needs to go on living. To work his way past whatever put that darkness into his eyes and find something worth living for, no matter how small a thing that might be."

Finished, Shayla looked at the chief of detectives hopefully, waiting for the man's decision.

Chapter 2

When the chief of detectives finally spoke, Brian Cavanaugh did so kindly and chose his words carefully.

"And you believe that you're the one who can help Detective Cortland step back from this abyss that you fear is threatening to swallow him up?" he asked the newest detective in his family.

Shayla never hesitated. It wasn't that she thought so much of herself—she just honestly thought that she could help the man who was so troubled he didn't even realize that he needed help.

"Yes, sir," she answered the chief. "I really believe that I can help Detective Cortland."

She saw the chief smile at her.

It was a known fact, a given, that all the Cavanaughs were good, decent people, but Brian had come to view

Shayla as practically goodness personified in the way
she went out of her way to try to help people, especially
the victims of crimes. If he were to place a bet on the
one person who could help the newly transferred detective to step back from the edge of the abyss, it would
most definitely be her.

Long ago Brian had made it a point to read the his-
tory of anyone who transferred into his police department. Cortland was no different. And while there were
glowing things cited about Cortland's abilities to track
down murderers, capturing killers who had heretofore
managed to elude being caught and bringing them in,
there was also a disturbing footnote in his file that
would back up Shayla's observation.

Which was why, although she was newly promoted
to the position of detective as well as new to the homicide division itself, Brian felt fairly comfortable assign-
ing her to be Cortland's partner.

If things didn't work out, Brian theorized, he could
always reassign Shayla to someone else. Heaven knew
they didn't lack for personnel when it came to any of
the departments.

"Well," Brian replied, "luckily, I think you can, too."

Unconsciously clutching the armrests, Shayla stared
at the chief of detectives. "Does that mean you're going
to assign me to be Cortland's partner?" she asked,
hardly able to believe that she had managed to convince the chief so easily. Family member or not, it usually took her a lot more words than this to get someone
to agree with her.

"For now, yes," Brian qualified. It was always a good idea to leave himself a way out if it became necessary.

The careful wording was not lost on Shayla. "And for later?" she couldn't help asking.

"Why don't we just see how this goes first?" he advised.

"Yes, of course," Shayla quickly agreed. She definitely didn't want to seem like she was offending the chief in any way. "Do you want me to find Cortland and tell him about this newest development?" she asked, ready and eager to volunteer for the assignment. The sooner this became a reality, the better.

Brian leaned back in his chair and could only laugh. "Lord, I don't remember any of the others being as eager as you," he told her, the others being the sum total of detectives he had dealt with ever since he had taken over his current position. According to everything he knew, Cortland and Shayla had never actually met. "Why don't you just stay here and leave the introductions to me? I just sent Cortland back down to the homicide division. Lieutenant Hollandale promised that he'd give Cortland a desk where he could set up."

"There aren't any," Shayla felt obligated to point out to the chief. "I got the last one last week."

Listening, the chief nodded, appearing unfazed. "I had another desk sent in just before you came in to request being partnered with Cortland." Anticipating Shayla's next question, he explained why an extra desk had just fortuitously turned up. "Detective Al Chapman retired from Missing Persons the other day. He took a security job position in the private sector," Brian explained and then smiled. "Seems his father-in-law owns the company. You know how it is, working for the family," the chief told her with a knowing wink. His father, Seamus Cavanaugh, onetime chief of police, just like Andrew had been, now ran his own security firm.

"Yes, sir, I am well acquainted with that sort of situation," Shayla answered, not bothering to suppress her smile.

Brian laughed softly to himself. All the Cavanaughs had dealt with snide remarks about privileged behavior because of their last name, but not a one of them had ever been known to actually capitalize on that, a fact that all the senior Cavanaughs were quite proud of.

The chief now nodded his head. "I thought you might be." Turning his chair slightly, he reached over to press a button on the phone on his desk. "Virginia, please call Lieutenant Hollandale for me. Ask him to send Detective Cortland back up to my office."

"What reason shall I give him, sir?" a disembodied, melodious voice asked. "In case he asks," his assistant added.

"Just that I would like to see him again," the chief said. His people didn't usually question why he wanted something to be done, and he was not in the habit of having to explain himself. His people had come to know that there were always good reasons behind anything he asked for.

"Consider it done, Chief," Virginia replied cheerfully.

Brian nodded to himself. He and his assistant had

had a good working relationship that spanned over the last decade. "I always do, Virginia," the chief answered.

Releasing the button on his phone, Brian looked over at the other occupant in his office. "When Cortland gets here, Shayla, I'd appreciate it if you let me make the introductions and do the talking to begin with. Cortland needs to know that the decision to team the two of you up came from me. As you might already suspect," he told her, "the new detective isn't overly keen on being partnered up with anyone. As a matter of fact, he specifically told me that he would rather *not* be assigned a partner."

"Did he give you any reason why?" she asked the chief.

"The usual one expressed by every loner I've ever met—he feels he works best alone," the chief replied. "So, if you want to change your mind—" Brian began.

She never gave the man the opportunity to finish. "I don't," Shayla replied emphatically.

Brian was not finished. "However, if for whatever reason, you come to the conclusion that this just isn't working for you—" the chief began again.

"I won't," she promised with feeling. "I'm determined to give this more than a day or two—or thirty," Shayla informed the chief with a wide smile.

Brian nodded. "Ah yes, I forgot how stubborn they told me you could be."

"'They'?" Shayla questioned. The man was exceptionally busy. When would he even have the time to discuss her with anyone?

"I believe that single word would encompass the entire family," he told her.

Just then, Virginia's voice came over the intercom. "He's here, Chief."

The chief briefly glanced in Shayla's direction before he told his assistant, "Send Detective Cortland in, please."

The next moment, there was just the slightest knock on the door. Shayla expected to see the door open and the detective who had been the topic of discussion come walking in.

But the door remained closed. Apparently, Detective Cortland was waiting to be told to come in.

The chief obliged. "Come on in, Detective Cortland."

The door opened, and the newest member of the Aurora detective squad walked into the chief's office.

Shayla couldn't pull her eyes away.

My Lord, she thought, *the man looks even handsomer close up than he did earlier at a distance.*

If nothing else, Cortland's presence was going to create a stir amid a great many of the detectives as well as the regular officers, she couldn't help thinking. Men *and* women—for different reasons.

Cortland looked exceedingly solemn. "Is there something you neglected to tell me, sir?" he asked, obviously at a loss as to why he had been called back.

Gabriel was aware that there was another person in the room, but since he assumed that she was just another member of the force and had nothing to do with him, he didn't spare her a glance or direct even a smattering of his attention toward her.

He was here because the chief had sent for him, no other reason.

Never an overly friendly man, he had completely withdrawn into himself after his wife, Natalie, had been killed. He had absolutely no interest in playing nice with any of the police personnel at large. He wasn't here to play nice. He was here to resume his pursuit of the Moonlight Killer. The serial killer who had exacted the ultimate payment from his wife.

"I wouldn't exactly say that I neglected to tell you something, Detective," Brian told the young man in response to Cortland's question. "But I have made a decision."

Shayla had been right, he caught himself thinking. Looking at the detective more closely now, it struck Brian that he had never seen such abject sadness in anyone's eyes before. Having Shayla around the detective might really do Cortland some good.

Gabriel waited for the chief to tell him what this decision he had made was all about. The detective had a very uneasy feeling that he knew, but given his pessimistic way of viewing things, he could be wrong, he thought.

He sincerely hoped so.

"I've decided to partner you up with another detective," Brian informed the newly transferred young man.

Surprise, displeasure and disbelief all briefly registered across Gabriel's ruggedly handsome face before fading away again just as quickly.

Gabriel cleared his voice. "I believe we already discussed that, sir," he politely told the chief, adding stiffly, "I don't do well with a partner."

Cortland briefly thought of the last man he had been partnered with. Jon Wakefield had been a decent enough partner in the beginning, but once Gabriel's world suddenly exploded and he sought relief at the bottom of a bottle, Wakefield had requested a different partner. Rather than realize what he was going through, Wakefield only focused on the way his drinking was interfering with their working relationship.

Angry, hurt, abandoned, Gabriel eventually resolved to drag himself back out of the tailspin that had sent him to a bottle for solace as well as relief from his pain.

Neither solace nor relief happened, but he was determined to stop drinking, so he went cold turkey and never looked back.

No one offered to help him achieve his goal of hunting down the man who had killed his wife—not that he would have listened to anyone had they tried. But it had just taught him that he couldn't count on anyone being there for him. The only one who ever had had been Natalie, and she had been cruelly taken from him.

A year ago, Gabriel had even been on the path to mellowing. Recently married, he was looking forward to becoming a father, becoming part of a real family. Abandoned by a mother who preferred partying to caring for her son, he'd been a loner for most of his life.

And then he had met Natalie, and for a while, he had begun to think that maybe things could change, maybe they could improve for him.

He should have known better.

Things never changed for the better—they only got worse. And he'd wound up paying the ultimate price for believing that happiness actually existed.

"I know what you said, Detective," the chief told him with an amiable smile, "but I decided that perhaps you would do better with a partner after all."

Gabriel made one last attempt to change the man's mind. "Sir, I don't—"

But Brian raised his hand, stopping the protest they both knew was about to come. "Why don't we give this a trial run?" Brian proposed. "Say, a month? A month from now, you can both come in and tell me how it's going."

For the first time since he had walked into chief's office, Gabriel slanted a glance toward the woman sitting in the chair next to his. "Both, sir?" he questioned.

Apparently their partnership had already been taken for granted, he realized, far from happy about the turn of events.

"Yes," Brian replied. "Detective Gabriel Cortland, I would like you to meet your new partner—" he gestured toward Shayla "—Detective Shayla Cavanaugh-O'Bannon."

Gabriel had heard only one word that had caught his attention in that introduction. "Cavanaugh, sir?"

Brian smiled. "Yes, the detective is part of my extended family. After you spend some time here, you'll discover that there are a great many of us here in the precinct. But don't let that get to you. The last name does not entitle any of them to any special treatment not awarded to other members of the force."

Shayla had extended her hand toward the detective the moment the chief had said her name. She was still holding it out toward Cortland, who seemed completely oblivious to the gesture.

It wasn't until the chief nodded in her direction that Gabriel seemed to realize that he had ignored the hand that had been extended to him by way of a greeting.

"Hi," Shayla said, smiling broadly. "Nice to meet you."

Relenting, Gabriel took her hand and shook it, holding it as if were some inanimate object he had been forced to pick up against his will. The connection was broken almost immediately as the detective grunted something in response.

Something that Shayla wasn't able to quite make out. Undoubtedly, she judged, it was not anything friendly. It didn't put her off. If anything, it just convinced her more than ever that the man needed her.

Her smile grew wider. "I am looking forward to working with you."

The look in Cortland's eyes when he briefly shifted them toward her told Shayla that she was alone in that sentiment.

"Well, that's all for now, Detectives," Brian said, his tone, although friendly, telling them that they were being dismissed. "Let me know how things are going in a month or so."

Cortland merely nodded at the chief as he rose and took his leave. Shayla was quick to follow, thinking that she certainly had her work cut out for her.

Brian was thinking the same thing as he watched the newly formed team leave his office. He really hoped that Shayla knew what she was getting herself into.

Chapter 3

Rather than ask the detective to shorten his stride—
Cortland had to be at least six inches taller than she was,
if not more, she thought—Shayla increased her stride
to the point that she was now almost trotting in order
to keep up with her new partner.

The low heels she was wearing were creating a stac-
cato beat as they quickly and rhythmically hit the floor
with each quick step she took. When she saw Cortland
about to pass the elevator doors, she realized that the
man was headed for the stairs.

"You know, if you're trying to lose me," she called
out to Cortland, glad more than ever that she ran on a
regular basis, "you're going to be doomed to failure. I
know the layout of this building a lot better than you
do, and even if your stride is wider and faster, I will

ultimately wind up in the same place that you do. So why don't you give up this race so we can walk into the homicide squad room at the same time like civilized people?"

Even as she made the suggestion, Shayla continued to trot behind Cortland like a stubborn racehorse in her last race, determined to at least make a good showing since winning the race was out of the question.

Gabriel Cortland stopped moving so suddenly, she almost found herself crashing into him. Shayla managed to catch herself at the very last moment.

Cortland glared down at her as if he couldn't believe she had said that. "You're assuming that I want to appear to be a civilized person."

"Don't you?" she questioned.

Still immobile, Gabriel continued looking down at her. This irritating thorn that had been inflicted on him didn't appear to be breathing hard, and she gave every appearance of being able to keep up this pace for at least a while longer.

Just his luck.

This, Gabriel caught himself thinking, had to be a brand-new high when it came to stubbornness.

"No," he finally bit off, answering her seemingly innocent question. "That would just be inviting interaction with other people here. I have no desire to interact or work with anyone." His vivid green eyes narrowed as he continued to glare at her, thinking that might get her to back off. "Least of all you."

Rather than be intimidated by him, he saw the annoyingly perky blonde actually smiling up at him.

"Sorry, but the chief wants us working together, so that means you're stuck with me, like it or not," she declared cheerfully. "And, between you and me, when you least expect it, you might actually find that you've grown to like it."

"I sincerely doubt that," he informed her coldly, thinking that between his tone and his expression, that should cut this annoying cheerful woman dead in her tracks.

It didn't.

"That's all right," Shayla countered his response. "When it happens, it'll be a surprise."

When the elevator arrived, he gave thought to darting in and boarding the car at the last moment, but that seemed somehow childish in his estimation, and that sort of behavior was reserved for her, not him.

So he walked into the elevator, averting his eyes and completely ignoring her.

At least, that was his plan, but he found it rather difficult to ignore someone who had obviously decided not to stop talking no matter what.

"I think you're going to like it here," Shayla predicted.

"You're entitled to your opinion," he told her in a removed voice that all but said her prediction didn't have a prayer of coming true.

Unfazed, Shayla continued. "Everyone's pretty friendly here."

"Doesn't matter," he informed her in a crisp but cold voice. "I'm not looking to make any friends."

"Sometimes things just happen even if you're not looking for them," she told him innocently.

His eyes swept over her, taking every single inch into account. For a pain in the neck, he had to admit that she was rather attractive—but attractive didn't interest him. Being left alone did.

"Tell me about it," he replied just as the elevator came to a stop.

The moment the doors parted, Gabriel immediately strode out. Shayla braced herself for another race.

To her surprise, this time Cortland did *not* stride ahead of her at a fast clip. The detective maintained a civilized pace that she was more than able to keep up with.

When he didn't suddenly take off, she flashed what he was beginning to think of as her blinding smile and said, "Thank you."

"For what, Cavanaugh?" he asked. To the best of his knowledge, he hadn't done anything for her to thank him about.

"For not making me trot all the way into the homicide squad," she told him. "And you can call me Shayla."

In no way could the look he spared her be classified as a warm one. "And why would I want to do that, Cavanaugh?" Cortland asked, deliberately emphasizing her last name.

Was everything going to be a contentious battle between them, she wondered.

"Because it's less of a mouthful than *Cavanaugh* is—and definitely less of a mouthful than the hyphenated version of my name." When he looked at her blankly, she explained, "Cavanaugh-O'Bannon. But whatever works for you is fine with me," Shayla concluded with a shrug that was meant to appease her new partner.

Gabriel narrowed his eyes practically into slits as he looked at her just before he turned away and walked into the thriving beehive that was the homicide squad.

"What would work for me, Cavanaugh," he informed her, "is working on my own."

She gave him an innocent, contrite look that almost looked believable.

Almost.

"Sorry," she went on to tell him. "We can't all get what we want." The smile she flashed in his direction looked as if it was wired for high voltage.

What Gabriel wanted was to be left alone, to do what he did in peace. But when he came right down to it, the only thing he *really* wanted was to catch the serial killer who had not only killed at least seventeen women and escaped capture but had thumbed his nose at him by killing the only person he had ever loved. A person who had been decent and pure and should have never even come in contact with a creature as demented and depraved as this serial killer was.

"Yes, I know," Gabriel answered in such a quiet, still voice that Shayla immediately knew that he wasn't referring to anything they had been talking about. This went a great deal deeper, was far more painful than anything that had, up until now, been touched upon even briefly.

What was it that tormented Cortland to this point?

For a moment, as she walked into the homicide squad room, Shayla briefly thought of going back to the chief and asking him what he knew about her new partner's background. But she knew that Brian Cavanaugh was very dedicated to the privacy of the men and women who worked for him. He sincerely believed that everyone was entitled to their secrets as long as those secrets did not ultimately hurt anyone else.

No, Shayla thought, if she wanted answers, she would have to look elsewhere. Not to the source, because she sincerely doubted that Cortland would tell her *anything* of that nature. He struck her as the very definition of the term *closemouthed*.

No, if she wanted answers, she had to find another way of delving into her new partner's past.

That was when her thoughts turned toward the computer.

Gabriel Cortland didn't strike her as someone who maintained even the barest minimum of a social media page, but that didn't mean there wasn't some sort of information about him floating around somewhere on the internet.

Almost *everything* was somewhere on the internet if a person just knew where to look or what files to access.

"Valri," she suddenly murmured out loud.

Shayla immediately pressed her lips together, afraid that Cortland had overheard her. But he apparently hadn't, because her unwilling new partner didn't even spare her a glance. Instead, his attention seemed to be focused on the man in the glass office at the extreme end of the squad room.

Lieutenant Dell Hollandale.

Relieved, Shayla went on mentally casting about for a solution. Which was why she had thought of Valri.

Valri Cavanaugh was one of two computer wizards in the family. If a fact could be located *anywhere* on the internet, even on the notorious dark web, Valri was the one who could find it. Shayla immediately made a mental note to talk to her cousin the first chance she got.

Right now, though, she felt that she needed to be at her new partner's side as the detective went through the motions of introducing himself to their lieutenant.

"Lieutenant Hollandale's office is that glass one all the way at the end of the squad room," Shayla pointed out.

Cortland gave her a look akin to the one he would have sent her way if she had just talked to him as if he was the village idiot.

"Yes, I know," Gabriel replied. "His assistant was the one who sent me back to the chief's office so I could be saddled with you."

She forced herself to ignore the obvious insult and focused on attempting to remedy the situation.

"You know," Shayla told the good-looking, brooding detective at her side, "if you think of this as a budding partnership rather than being 'saddled' with me, it might be easier for you to come to terms with this."

The expression on his face told her he didn't see it that way. "What would be easier for me is if you changed your mind and asked for another partner," Cortland told her matter-of-factly.

She was not about to lie to him, not even to attempt

to get along with the man. He needed to accept the situation as it existed.

"That's not about to happen," she said with a smile.

"And neither is my thinking of this—" he gestured to the space between them, pointing toward her and then himself "—as a partnership."

Not about to accept defeat, but unwilling to hash this all out right now, Shayla promised, "We'll revisit this later."

Gabriel made no immediate reply. He knew that he needed to remain in this precinct, and it wasn't in his best interest to lose his temper in front of the entire squad on his first day on the job.

He made his way across the floor to the lieutenant's office. Just before he was about to knock on the glass door, he glanced at the woman at his side. "We'll see," he told her.

The next moment, Cortland was knocking on Hollandale's door. There was no more time for any sort of an exchange between him and the incredibly annoying woman at his side.

While he didn't paste a smile on his face, Gabriel did do his best to look unperturbed, at least for his first meeting with his new superior.

"Ah, Detective Cortland and Detective Cavanaugh, I take it you've met one another," Hollandale said, rising from behind his desk to extend a hand to each detective, although he had obviously already met Shayla.

"Just barely, sir," Shayla answered, slanting a look toward her new partner.

"Yes, sir," Cortland answered stoically.

"I've read your file, Cortland," Hollandale said, sitting down again. He nodded for the detectives to do the same, then continued. "Your superiors had some very impressive things to say about you," he observed. "And yet you transferred." He raised his penetrating brown eyes to the detective's face. "Why?"

The answer, in Gabriel's opinion, couldn't have been simpler. "The serial killer I have been pursuing over the last two years suddenly changed his hunting grounds, switching from Los Angeles to Aurora and the surrounding area. I didn't think the Aurora police department would look kindly on an LA police detective pushing his way into their—your—investigation."

It wasn't the entire truth, but Gabriel felt that it would satisfy his new boss. Solved cases far outweighed everything else.

Hollandale continued looking at the new detective. "Is that the only reason?" he asked.

Shayla found herself hanging on every word being exchanged between the two men. She wondered if Cortland would open up or continue repeating the known facts.

Cortland took a breath, then said, "Things in Los Angeles became rather intolerable for me. It was time for a change. Luckily, as it turned out, it came at a good time for the ongoing investigation as well."

"What makes you think that the killer moved here?" Hollandale asked. "He could have easily taken off for another state."

"He didn't," Cortland replied with conviction.

Hollandale wasn't quite ready to drop the matter. He

wanted to be convinced, or at least understand what had made Cortland believe what he did.

"What makes you so sure?"

"Call it a gut feeling," Gabriel replied evasively.

Shayla looked at the detective in surprise. She hadn't expected this sort of an admission from someone who behaved more like a sphinx than a human being.

"You have a gut feeling?" she questioned.

Gabriel felt as if she was talking down to him. One look at the woman's face disproved that, but it was still difficult for him to give her the benefit of the doubt.

However, the lieutenant's office was not the place to allow his dismissive feelings toward this partner he had been saddled with to surface.

So all he allowed himself to say was, "Yes, I have a gut feeling."

Shayla smiled. He noted that it wasn't a mocking smile but a pleased one. The woman was up to something.

"As someone who comes from a family that has made gut feelings into a religion," Shayla told him, "I think that going with a gut feeling is an excellent way to proceed."

Gabriel really thought that this time the bouncy detective was making fun of him. However, a closer look at the woman told him she was serious. He realized that he had stopped talking to his new lieutenant and had shifted his attention to the annoying detective who had somehow managed to latch onto him for reasons that were hers alone.

He had to be crazy, he told himself. And it was her

fault. She had burrowed into his life in less than a half an hour, and already he felt as if his life was being turned on its ear.

How the hell had that happened, anyway?

It was the serial killer who needed his undivided attention, not some dippy, privileged little princess who was the unfortunate by-product of what seemed like an otherwise extremely bright, capable family.

Well, with any luck, she would get tired of whatever game she thought she was playing and would request another partner, leaving him alone to do what he had come out to do: rid the world of a serial killer and live up to the promise he had made at Natalie's grave.

To kill the man who had killed her.

Chapter 4

"Well, for the city's sake, I hope this guy doesn't turn up anywhere near here," the lieutenant said to the two people in his office. "But, on the other hand, we're never going to catch that sick SOB by sticking our heads in the sand while keeping our fingers crossed that he stays away." Hollandale's normally easygoing expression turned momentarily dark. "That scum has to be brought down—and as soon as possible."

Shayla glanced toward Cortland and decided to answer for both of them, since the latter wasn't being very vocal. "You're preaching to the choir, sir."

"I realize that," the lieutenant answered. Looking at the newest detective on his squad, Hollandale said, "I assume that when you were working the serial killer cases, you kept records."

"I did, yes," Gabriel answered.

Hollandale eyed him a little closer. "Detailed records?" he emphasized.

"I'd like to think so," Gabriel replied honestly, without any fanfare.

"And would you have kept any copies of those detailed records when you moved out here?" Hollandale asked.

Gabriel paused, wondering if this was a legitimate question or if his new lieutenant was attempting to trip him up for some reason. Ordinarily, when a detective left a precinct, the files he had worked on remained behind, because they were the property of that precinct. Technically, he had no business bringing those files with him, but everyone knew that copies of notes had a habit of turning up in places where they normally didn't belong.

"I don't believe that I still have any of those files, sir." That would have been the standard, expected denial. But because he was honest to a fault, Gabriel threw in a proviso. "However, I would have to look through my papers to make sure."

Hollandale nodded his head at the nonadmission. "Do that as soon as you get a chance," he encouraged. "In the meantime, settle in and get to know the people you'll be working with. You'll both be complaining that you don't have time to even breathe soon enough," the lieutenant assured them with conviction. "Detectives Joan Mateo and Greg Jordan are just wrapping up a murder-suicide case. You might want to look over their shoulder and see how we handle things here," Hollandale suggested, looking directly at Cortland as he said it.

Shayla took that to be their cue to leave and rose to her feet.

"Yes, sir," she responded, then looked at Cortland to see if he was getting up as well. The latter seemed to stand almost reluctantly.

"Sir," he began, searching for a way to state what had occurred to him without sounding pushy or being thought of as offensive.

One of the by-products of having taken over this job, the lieutenant had learned, was developing the patience of a saint. "Yes?" Hollandale asked.

"If a killing does come up that matches the LA Moonlight Killer's pattern—" Gabriel began.

Cortland didn't have to finish his request. The lieutenant knew where this was going, and he nodded at the detective. Cortland's knowledge of the serial killer's pattern was one of the reasons the man had been welcomed to the homicide division of the Aurora police department.

"I will be sure to call the two of you in," he assured Cortland.

"The two of us?" Gabriel questioned. For the briefest of moments, he had forgotten all about the albatross hung around his neck.

"Yes. Detective Cavanaugh is, after all, your partner," Hollandale reminded the new man. "Or did you forget that?" he asked, amusement curving his mouth.

Gabriel felt like a man who had been placed on a

medieval torture rack and had somehow managed to pass out, temporarily forgetting where he was.

"It slipped my mind for a minute, sir," Cortland admitted.

Hollandale actually chuckled as he looked at Shayla. "I am sure Cavanaugh will be happy to keep reminding you, Detective."

"I'm sure she will," Cortland agreed darkly. The humor in the situation, as seen by his lieutenant, escaped him.

"Well, that's all for now," Hollandale said with a note of finality in his voice. He spared the new detective another smile. "Welcome to the unit, Detective Cortland."

"Thank you, sir," Gabriel murmured politely, feeling as if he had just officially walked through the gates of hell.

"Well, that went well," Shayla cheerfully commented as they came out of the lieutenant's office.

Gabriel merely grunted something completely unintelligible in response.

"I'm going to need a handbook on how to interpret those grunts of yours," she told her partner honestly. "Was that a good grunt or an indifferent grunt?"

"You're the detective, you tell me," Cortland said.

She sidestepped what she viewed as a trap. "I'm going to need more input before I can form an intelligent opinion," Shayla answered. "What I can tell you right off the bat is that I'm your friend, Cortland. At times, when we're out in the field, I might be your only friend. And I will have your back each and every time. But you are going to have to stop viewing me as the enemy, because that is the one thing I am not.

"Now, that's your desk over there." She pointed toward the newly placed piece of furniture that, as it happened, was right in front of hers, although she didn't tell him that yet.

Cortland was going to love this, she couldn't help thinking. The next moment, the look on his face told her she was right.

Out loud, Shayla suggested, "Why don't you settle in, and once you finish doing that, I can introduce you around."

"Why would you do that?" Gabriel asked suspiciously.

It looked as if this partner of hers was going to fight her every step of the way. Well, she had asked for this, so she couldn't really complain about it, she reminded herself.

"Because," she explained patiently, "these are the people you're going find yourself working with at one point or another."

"I've got a better idea," Gabriel countered. "Why don't we wait until that time comes up before you start playing the hostess with the mostest?"

Okay, she thought. She needed Cortland to back off a little before she found herself losing the temper she was striving so hard to hold on to.

"I want to make one thing very clear," she told Cortland. "I grew up with three bossy, overbearing older brothers and a whole bunch of obnoxious male cousins. More than you could possibly shake a stick at. If I didn't kill any of them then and am on good terms with all of them now, you don't have a prayer of driving me off with your less-than-amiable behavior," she informed him point-blank.

"So you might as well give it up, because, barring an earthquake where the ground opens up right under my feet and swallows me whole, I am *not* going anywhere."

Her eyes met his, and for the first time since he had met the woman, Gabriel noticed that her eyes were a vivid shade of light blue.

"Have I made myself clear?" Shayla asked.

"Yes," Cortland replied, his lips barely moving.

Her smile was as wide as his frown was pronounced. "Great!" she declared. Gesturing toward the empty desk again, she told him, "There's your desk."

He retreated to it as if it was his last bastion of refuge. The next moment, that notion was totally sacrificed when he saw her sit down at the desk that was right beside the one he had just been directed to.

The scowl on his face resurfaced and looked even more intense than it had just a little earlier. Shayla pretended not to notice. The detective was going to need time to adjust, she thought.

Probably more than the usual amount.

But she had absolutely no doubt that Cortland *would* adjust, because she had no intentions of giving up, and, as her mother had once noted—rather proudly when she thought that she hadn't been overheard by her daughter—her youngest child could be stubborn as hell when she wanted to be.

And however briefly she'd been in Cortland's company, Shayla most definitely intended to be *very* stubborn and wait out this deeply hurting detective.

Shayla gave her new partner an hour to settle in, and then, because they hadn't been placed on an actual case yet, she began to slowly bring some of the older detectives by Cortland's desk.

Granted, she was a newly promoted homicide detective, but she knew almost all the people there thanks to having interacted with them both on the force and at any one of her uncle Andrew's numerous gatherings and parties.

Among other things, it bred a sense of camaraderie within the police force. Practically everyone chipped in to defray what could have been a prohibitive cost if the former chief of police had to bear the expense on his own.

Consequently, relatives and friends were more than happy to contribute. The real draw to these parties, other than the company, was the way Andrew cooked. Cooking had been a passion of his when he was putting himself through school. It only grew more so as the years went by.

To Cortland's credit, he didn't actually say anything to show that he had no interest in broadening his circle of acquaintances. But his body language did seem to reinforce that particular message.

"Your new partner isn't exactly sunshine in a bottle, is he?" Brianna commented at one point after her sister introduced Cortland to her. A few seconds later, the detective had excused himself and retreated.

Feeling somewhat protective toward the man, Shayla said, "It takes him time to warm up to people."

"Are you sure he's capable of warming up?" her sister

asked skeptically. "Hell, I've seen icebergs melt faster than your new partner."

"He's dealing with some things," Shayla replied. She only wished she knew what, she added silently.

"We're *all* dealing with some things, Shay. There's no reason to give anyone frostbite when they make the mistake of walking by," Brianna told her. And then her tone softened as she looked at Shayla. "I don't want to see you put yourself out there and get hurt, kid."

"Hurt?" Shayla repeated with a scoff. "Haven't you heard, Bri? I'm invulnerable."

"Yeah, yeah." Brianna waved her hand, humoring Shayla because she knew there was no way to talk her sister out of doing something once she had set her mind to it. "Look, in honor of you being the last of us to pass the detectives' exam," Brianna said, doing her best not to grin, "why don't you come down to Malone's and join us all for a celebratory drink?"

It was just after hours now, and none of the inner group were out working a case at the moment. To Brianna it seemed like the perfect time to get all of them together.

"Sure. Just let me go and ask Cortland if he wants to join us," Shayla said.

She turned toward where she had last seen her new partner.

Brianna scanned the immediate area. "Doesn't look as if he is, kid," she told her younger sister. "I think your new partner just ducked out when you weren't looking and went home."

Shayla began to protest, but she saw that Cortland's desk was empty.

And he was nowhere to be seen.

Brianna was right.

Doing nothing was a great deal more tiring than actually working a case, Gabriel thought angrily. He had forgotten that.

He let out a long breath as he walked into his sparsely furnished ground-floor garden apartment. It wasn't home, but it was a refuge, he thought. And that was all he was interested in.

Because of that incessantly chipper partner he had been saddled with, he had begun to feel as if today was just never going to end. It was just going to go on and on like a merry-go-round whose mechanism had gotten stuck and somehow was doomed to continue, having him go around and around in an endless circle until he eventually expired.

It was days like today that made him really regret giving up drinking. Having a tall, cold Black Russian would have really gone down well right about now.

He took down an all but empty box of crackers and extracted the last of them. Bringing the box over to the sofa, he began to dispose of the last of the crackers. They were stale.

He thought longingly again of a Black Russian. It would have been an easy enough matter just to go to a local bar or restaurant and order one. But he knew he couldn't give in, not even for a single drink, because it was *never* a single drink. One drink would lead to another and another until he was right back to where he had been nine months ago.

After he had found Natalie's body, he had tried so desperately to find a way to cope with the pain, to mute it, drown it, do something, *anything* to make it stop haunting his every waking moment. So he had a choice between being haunted or being a hopeless drunk who couldn't cope with life.

Hell of a choice, he thought as he ate another stale cracker.

The bottle had come incredibly close to winning him over to its side but giving in to that sort of an existence was an insult to his late wife on several levels. Natalie wouldn't have wanted him to devolve to this state.

More importantly, if he gave in to his pain and drowned his sorrows to the point that he was incapable of even thinking, how could he ever make that disgusting subhuman who had done this to Natalie pay for what he had done? Pay for stealing not just the rest of her life, but their baby's life as well?

Not to mention their life as a family?

But to do that, to capture the serial killer, he had to remain sober. Not just occasionally, but at all times.

And once he had tracked this ruthless creature down and made him pay the ultimate price for what he had done—not just to his beloved Natalie and their unborn child, but to all the women he had killed and the families he had robbed of their presence—once he had done that, Gabriel didn't care what happened to him. He would have done what he needed to do.

The rest of his life after that didn't matter to him. Because without Natalie, there was no life for him.

Gabriel pressed his lips together, wishing he could have just one single drink. But that wasn't possible, which was why he didn't bring any alcohol into the apartment he had rented. Not even to help him sleep.

Sleepless nights had become the norm for him, but he has gotten used to them. All he needed was just enough time to recharge and he could keep going.

The knock on his door had him stiffening. He'd lived here for almost a month and knew absolutely no one.

So who the hell was that?

Chapter 5

Because the person at his front door wasn't showing any signs of going away despite his inclination to ignore them—whoever was there had already knocked a total of three times—Gabriel decided he needed to make them leave.

Muttering under his breath, he stormed over to the front door.

At first, when he looked through the peephole, Gabriel thought his imagination had gotten the better of him. Cavanaugh had relentlessly been dogging his tracks ever since the chief had given him the bad news that he was teaming the two of them up.

Seeing Cavanaugh standing on the other side of his door now was just a continuation of the nightmare he felt he was having.

Except, apparently, it wasn't a nightmare, because, no matter how much he blinked and willed her gone, she was still standing there.

"Cortland," Shayla said, "I know you can see me. I can hear you breathing."

"I'm off duty, Cavanaugh. We're done for the day," he informed her curtly.

But Shayla stood her ground. The dinner she had brought with her from Malone's was beginning to cool. She needed to give it to him now.

"Open your door, please, Cortland."

The door remained closed with its lock in place. "Why should I?" he asked. Didn't this woman ever give up and stop making a pest of herself? What the hell had he done to be plagued like this?

"Because I'll make it worth your while, Cortland," she promised.

He sighed, debating what to do. He could ignore her. It wasn't easy, but it could be done. However, if he didn't let her in, this nutcase was liable to stand out there all night, making noise and talking endlessly. Eventually, one of the neighbors was going to get irritated enough to call 911 and complain.

Gabriel swore under his breath. That was all he needed.

Flipping the lock, he yanked open the door, but he didn't hold it open all the way. His arm was up, barring her access. "What are you doing here?" he demanded angrily.

Ignoring the fact that he hadn't exactly invited her

in, Shayla ducked under his arm and wiggled her way into his apartment.

A warm, tempting smell accompanied her.

"You haven't eaten, have you?" she asked, turning around to face him. It wasn't really a question on her part but more of an assumption.

"Now you're answering a question with a question?" Gabriel asked. Frowning, he closed the door, but he didn't flip the lock into place. He wanted to be able to pull it open quickly.

"It's not really a question," she confessed. "It's more like intuition." She looked pointedly at the almost empty container of stale crackers in his hand. "And the fact that I didn't see you eat anything all day."

"I wasn't hungry." His eyes narrowed as he all but pinned her in place. "Something kept killing my appetite."

"Well, sorry to hear that," she responded with an innocent expression, "but I figured that your appetite might have made a reappearance by now, so I brought you a thick steak sandwich from Malone's as well as a bag of their fries."

"Malone's?" Gabriel was unfamiliar with the name. Actually, he was unfamiliar with most of the different places in Aurora. He had even chosen the apartment where he was currently living solely because of its proximity to the police precinct. To Gabriel, being able to roll out of bed and go directly to work was a major plus. He was not interested in the scenery.

Shayla had taken the wrapped sandwich and fries

out of the bag and placed them on the small table in his equally small kitchen.

Flattening the bag, she held it up for him to see the Malone's logo.

"It's a local bar and grill run by a retired detective. Actually, everyone who works there used to be with the police force," she added. "You should come down sometime." Her face lit up at the thought. "I can take you there."

If he told her not to come, Gabriel sensed that wouldn't be enough to put the woman off, so he told her shortly, "I'm not planning to have any time for that."

"You can't work all the time," she told him, thinking about the old saying that all work and no play made for a dull person. Shayla pressed her lips together, deciding that saying so out loud could probably just lead to an argument that she didn't want to have right now.

He focused on what she had just said about his not being able to work all the time. His eyes narrowed, taking it as a challenge. "Try me," Cortland told her.

"Right now, I think you should try the steak sandwich," Shayla urged, deliberately changing the topic. "It tastes good cold, but it's even better warm."

It did smell good, Gabriel thought almost against his will. The tempting aroma just reminded him that stale crackers for dinner didn't quite cut it. But he wasn't about to have this bossy little fresh-out-of-the-box detective telling him when and what to eat.

And he *really* wanted to get her out of his apartment.

"Maybe later," he told her as he took a step back toward the front door

But Shayla didn't move. She remained exactly where she was and nodded toward the food she had placed on the table.

"Let's just say that you're not getting rid of me until I see you eating." She deliberately didn't phrase her statement to say, "Start eating." She wanted the process to include finishing the meal, otherwise, she wouldn't put it past him to stubbornly throw the food out.

She could see by the look on Cortland's face that he was definitely considering that unspoken option.

"You really do know how to make a pest of yourself, don't you?" Cortland said, stunned by her behavior and, at the same time, rather surprised by her single-mindedness. It occurred to him that she would be a driven detective if she applied that same stubbornness to a case she was on.

Rather than be insulted that Cortland had called her a pest, Shayla smiled complacently at him and said, "I have a PhD in it."

Gabriel came close to laughing. "I just bet you do," he answered. Turning on his heel, Gabriel spared his annoying partner a glance and said, "Well, c'mon," and then walked into the small kitchen.

Buoyed and hopeful, Shayla followed.

Against the wall there was the small table where she'd placed the sandwich and fries. Three chairs surrounded the table. Cortland took a seat directly opposite the one that Shayla slipped into.

"Good?" she asked after Cortland had had a chance to take a couple of bites of his sandwich.

The sandwich was still warm, but Gabriel just shrugged. "It's okay," he said in between more bites.

"I'll pass that heady praise of yours to Reese, who currently does all the cooking at Malone's. I'll just make sure all the knives and meat cleavers are out of reach before I say anything," she confided, a smile playing on her lips.

Sharp green eyes narrowed ever so slightly as Gabriel looked at her. "Is sarcasm your first language or your second?" he asked.

"Second," she answered without hesitation. "Being around certain types of people just seems to bring it out of me," she said innocently. And then, still looking up at him, Shayla promised, "I'll try to keep a lid on it."

Gabriel shrugged again, trying not to allow his irritation to surface. Ever since Natalie had been killed, he'd had trouble holding on to his temper. It was better now than when he was drinking, but it still wasn't the way it used to be.

"Suit yourself," he told her.

"I usually do," she answered honestly. "But I also like taking the people around me into account."

He found himself wondering again if she was on the level. "Must get tiring," he noted.

"At times," she agreed. She was still looking at him pointedly. "But at other times it can be extremely satisfying." She sat back and continued to watch him eat.

Gabriel realized he was waiting for her to stop. To grow tired of being this cheerful Pollyanna and allow her true colors to finally surface. This woman had been perpetuating this act all day, and even people pretending to be Santa Claus had to give it a rest eventually, right?

But this eager beaver seemed to enjoy this act she had been playing all day, and she gave no sign of stopping or even of backing off the tiniest bit.

"You seem really invested in having me finish every last bite," Gabriel noted. "Is that when the cyanide kicks in?" he asked sarcastically.

"No, not until a day or two later," she answered with such a straight face, for a second Gabriel actually thought that she was being serious.

And then she started to laugh, giving herself away and, coincidentally, annoying the hell out of him.

"That wasn't funny," he informed her icily.

"Neither is treating me like the enemy or some invading force," Shayla countered. Pausing, she told herself to regroup. "Look, why don't we both return to our corners and start over?"

For the sake of getting along, she had placed herself in with him, but in her honest opinion, her grumpy partner was the only one who needed to return to his corner and start over.

But she wasn't here to judge him, Shayla reminded herself. She was here to try to win him over and make him realize that she wasn't just his partner. She could be his friend if he only let his guard down a little and let her in.

When Cortland made no response, she leaned in a little, reached up to take hold of an imaginary bell and said, "Ding, ding, ding."

He frowned at her. Maybe it was her imagination,

but the frown didn't seem quite as intense as it had been initially. *Progress?* she thought hopefully.

"You missed your calling," Cortland told her. "Maybe you should be doing voice-overs in cartoons."

"Maybe," Shayla replied, nodding as if she was giving the idea some thought.

He watched her for a long moment, unable to understand her motives any more now than he had when she had first arrived. "I take it this is what people mean when they refer to bending over backward," Cortland guessed.

"I wouldn't know," she replied innocently. "I'm not bending."

The expression on his face was the last word in skepticism. She was kidding, right? Still, he asked, "So this is normal behavior for you?"

Her smile was almost blinding. "Now you're learning," she told him.

He realized that he had almost eaten the whole sandwich—and it had been exceptionally thick, as well as good. But what really bothered him was that the food—and his no longer empty stomach—had managed to distract him.

He never should have opened the door.

"Look," he started, "I don't know what your game is, but—"

"I already told you this morning when we were first introduced. There is no game. All I care about is working with you and, just possibly, if we do it right, making this small part of the world a better, safer place for the people who are in it." Shayla's eyes met his. "Nothing else really matters."

She was some actress, he thought. Another man might have believed her. But another man hadn't been through what he had.

"And you expect me to believe that?" he challenged.

Shayla's eyes never wavered from his. "Yes," she replied, "I do. Maybe not today or tomorrow or even the next day, but eventually. Because it's true."

Cortland grunted just the way he had done earlier in the office. *Nobody* was this sunny, he thought. *Nobody.*

"And if you happen to cut your finger, is sugar going to come pouring out?" he asked.

He was goading her. It was hard to keep the smile on her face, but she managed even as she rose to her feet.

"I really wouldn't recommend doing that to see if you're right," she told him.

It took him a second to realize that she was heading toward the door. He had wanted her to do that since she had arrived, yet now that it looked as if it was really happening, he almost couldn't believe it.

Belatedly, he came to and followed her, walking his so-called partner to the door a step behind her.

"Well, thanks for the steak sandwich—and the fries." His own voice sounded almost awkward to him.

"My pleasure," she answered, her tone bright again. "I figured there was no advantage in having a partner whose stomach was rumbling at inopportune times."

Gabriel took offense at the offhanded comment. "My stomach wasn't rumbling," he informed her.

"It was only a matter of time," she promised. "Don't

forget, I did grow up with all those brothers and cousins. I am well acquainted with the sounds of hunger, and to the best of my recollection, you hadn't eaten."

"I could have gotten something to eat after I left the precinct," he pointed out.

"Then I wouldn't have found you with a container of stale crackers in your hand," she told him.

Now she was just reaching. "How would you even know they were stale?" he asked.

"The noise they made when you bit into one," she answered cheerfully. "Fresh crackers sound different from stale ones."

"And you've investigated crackers?" Cortland asked cynically.

She didn't answer him directly. "It's all just part of conducting intense investigations," she informed him. "You never know when one small piece of information can suddenly fit in and make everything else just click into place." She glanced at her watch. "Now, it's getting late, and I should go so you can get some sleep."

He stared at her. Just how old did she think he was? "It's not even eight o'clock."

"I know, but it probably takes you a long time to finally fall asleep. I had better leave so that you can get started."

His sleeping patterns had been off for the last nine months. He couldn't fall asleep for hours, and when he finally did, nightmares would quickly materialize and haunt him. He would wake up feeling even more tired than when he had finally fallen asleep.

But he had never told anyone that. He wasn't the kind

to share. This partner of his was getting to be downright creepy.

"How would you know that?" Gabriel asked.

"You have bags under your eyes. The kind that come from lack of sleep. Since you're currently not working a case, there's only one thing that could keep you up—your own thoughts. And those are hard to bury," she told him knowingly. The next moment, she opened his door. "See you tomorrow, partner," she said cheerfully as she slipped out the door.

Cavanaugh was an annoying, pushy woman who had managed, in the matter of just hours, to get under his skin like some sort of infectious rash, Gabriel thought as he watched her go.

And, he supposed, judging by her conclusions, she also seemed like she had the makings of a half-decent detective.

Biting off an oath, Gabriel flipped the lock on his door, closing it.

Unless the woman had learned how to slip under the door like some sort of witch, that should keep her out, he decided.

Chapter 6

Gabriel arrived at the precinct the next morning at seven thirty. It wasn't so much that he was eager to get started. Oddly enough, the quiet in his apartment after his chatty pseudopartner had left began to get to him. Every sound seemed to be amplified.

He could hear his ears ringing.

Gabriel had thought of putting on the television in order to have some background noise, but there was nothing on except for either inane programs that insulted his intelligence or sickeningly "clever" newscasters who thought they were entertaining because they were bantering back and forth while making little sense.

At that point, Gabriel had given up and just gone to bed.

Going to bed turned out to be another futile endeavor

for him. Not for lack of trying, Gabriel had managed to get in about five hours of sleep. Not straight through, but in broken snatches.

The last time he woke up, he figured he was done for the night. Because he was, he decided to go in earlier than he was actually scheduled to come in.

Aurora was known as one of the more peaceful, law-abiding cities in the country. Still, he reasoned, there had to be *something* happening now that he could sink his teeth into.

And, if he hadn't missed his guess, this city was exactly the type of setting that the Moonlight Killer, as he had been dubbed by some journalist, was looking for in order to leave his new mark.

The heartless ghoul enjoyed nothing better than bringing fear into the hearts of heretofore peaceful people.

Because of the proximity of his apartment to the precinct as well as the lack of traffic, Gabriel managed to make it from his apartment to the precinct in no time flat.

The homicide squad room was practically empty when he walked in.

Or so it looked at first glance.

And then Gabriel stopped dead.

Apparently nightmares continue even when you're awake, Gabriel thought, seeing his partner already at her desk.

Approaching Shayla, he asked, "What are you doing here?"

Shayla had barely made it in a few minutes earlier,

managing to get an abbreviated run in before taking a quick shower. Pleased with herself, she looked up at her partner, a hint of an amused smile curving her mouth.

"I work here, remember?"

Oh, he remembered all right, Gabriel thought. He had thought—hoped, really—that by coming in so early, he would be able to avoid her for at least an hour, possibly longer. Obviously, he had thought wrong.

"I know," he answered formally. "But you don't work this early."

"Actually," she told him, "I like getting an early start." Shayla nodded toward her computer screen. "I decided to read everything I could find about that serial killer in LA and the surrounding area. By the way, that coffee is for you," she said, tilting her head at the large, covered container standing in the middle of his desk.

He hadn't even noticed it. She had been what had caught his attention, front and center. "Where did it come from?" Cortland asked.

"Well, if I said the coffee fairy, you probably wouldn't believe me," Shayla laughed, "so why don't we just say that it came from the coffee shop at the end of the block?"

He made no move to pick up the container. Instead, he continued just looking at it with suspicion. "What's it doing here?"

"Standing?" she supplied, amused.

"Damn it, Cavanaugh—" The woman had just managed to make him lose his temper in record time, he thought, frustrated.

"Ask a stupid question, you force me to give you a

stupid answer," Shayla said, then decided to tell him the truth. "I stopped to get my morning coffee at the shop and decided that you might want something a little stronger than the discolored dishwater that passes for coffee around here." She looked into his eyes. "I am trying to make this as hospitable a workplace as possible for you, but you're going to have to work with me a little here."

"I didn't ask you to do that." Gabriel stopped.

He had to get hold of himself or he would wind up being fired before he had a chance to even start working at this precinct. There was no getting away from the gut feeling that the fiend who had stolen Natalie from him was going to bring his killing spree here next—if he hadn't already.

He couldn't explain why—he just *knew*.

So Cortland forced himself to reel in his temper and did his best to sound civilized. "Sorry. Thank you. What do I owe you?" he asked, reaching for his wallet.

"I'll take a smile," Shayla told him cheerfully.

His eyes met hers. "You don't give up, do you?"

She grinned in response. "Ah, you're learning." Cortland's expression appeared almost frozen, and then, slowly, there was just the slightest movement at the corners of his mouth. "I guess that's good for a first effort," Shayla told him, nodding her approval. "After all, you can only go up from there."

With that, she lowered her eyes and looked back at her computer screen.

Working diligently, she had managed to find a number of stories about the serial killer, each one more bone-chilling than the last.

The killings, she discovered, all appeared to have been committed in the evening, and oddly enough, none of the victims had been sexually assaulted.

Then there was the fact that all the bodies had been tied up in that same painful, hog-tied fashion.

After reading the tenth story, sickened, Shayla had had to stop for a second.

She blew out a breath, shaking her head.

"What?" Cortland asked, curious as to what seemed to have gotten to her.

She realized that her partner was sitting at his desk, drinking his coffee and watching her. Was he trying to get a handle on her reaction, she wondered, or was there something else going on? She didn't have a clue. Cortland wasn't the easiest man to read.

"By definition," she said, answering his vaguely worded question, "serial killers are all sick people, but this one, it's like he goes out of his way to be particularly sick."

Gabriel certainly wasn't about to argue with that. "Yeah."

Cortland's voice sounded painfully flat to her, as if he didn't just agree with her assessment, he felt it all the way down to his bones.

Shayla glanced at the date of the last article she had read, which apparently was about the serial killer's last victim.

"Am I reading this right? This ghoul hasn't surfaced for the last nine months?" she asked her partner.

"Yeah, you're right," he answered curtly.

It had been nine months, he thought. Nine months ago when his life came to a painful, skidding halt and the walls of his life came crashing in on him. It was also the last time that anyone had supposedly heard from the Moonlight Killer.

Shayla was studying the screen. "There're a lot of reasons why the killer would just disappear from the scene," she said, thinking out loud. "Someone could have killed him and his body hasn't been discovered yet. Or he moved on to another city or state to continue his killing spree.

"Or," she speculated further, "he could have been arrested for some unrelated crime and is currently serving time in prison right now." These were just some of the things that had been known to happen to other killers, causing them to disappear from the scene and keep them from conducting what they felt driven to do.

Cortland waited for her to pause, then said, "Maybe."

"But you don't think so," Shayla guessed, observing his expression.

He was not about to say he had a gut feeling again. In his opinion, saying so the first time had been a mistake on his part. Even though she said he shared that instinct with some of her family, he felt it made him appear foolish.

So he flippantly said, "Fortune-telling is not in my realm."

"Not mine, either," she answered. "Just making a calculated guess based on past events. Enjoy your coffee," she told him, ending what she felt had become a stilted conversation at best.

Shayla went back to reading through the various serial killer stories, because, unfortunately, there were more.

But she couldn't keep her mind on what she was reading. The stories were upsetting, to say the least, and she had to admit that she was being distracted by her new partner. Not because of anything he had said specifically so much as the unsettling vibes she was picking up.

The man had been through hell, and he didn't give her the impression he was back yet. She needed to find out what had happened to him. How could she have his back if she didn't know what was going on?

Shayla had already decided that asking Cortland about it wasn't going to get her anywhere except insanely frustrated, and going to the chief of detectives would bring her to the same dead end.

What she needed was input from a friendly source.

She had thought of Valri yesterday and hadn't had a chance to touch base with her cousin yet. Maybe it was time to do that.

Rising, she stopped by Cortland's desk. "I'll be right back," she promised.

Leafing through a report that had been on his desk when he came in this morning, Gabriel shrugged.

"Take all the time you want," he told her.

Shayla couldn't resist telling him, "Try not to miss me," before she headed for the squad room doorway.

The expression in his eyes when he raised them told her that he definitely wouldn't.

Shayla walked faster. If she discovered that there was nothing responsible for those sad eyes of his and he just had a nasty disposition, she promised herself that Cortland was going to be a very, very sorry human being.

Shayla took the elevator down to the basement, where both the morgue and the computer research department were located—fortunately not next to one another.

The door to the computer research department was open. There appeared to be several people in the room, but she didn't hear any voices. What she did hear was the rhythmic clicking of computer keys.

Stepping just inside the large, square room, Shayla knocked on the side of the door.

Valri was located on the far side of the room, completely involved in what she was doing. She usually was.

Even so, alert to any different sound, the computer expert raised her eyes in response to the knock.

"Hi!" Shayla greeted the woman everyone who availed themselves of her services referred to as "the computer wizard."

"Are you busy right now, Valri?"

She knew the woman obviously was, but it was a way for her to initiate the conversation she needed to have.

Humor played across Valri's lips. "Compared to me, Santa Claus is sitting still, twiddling his thumbs. Why? What is it that you want me to do that I can't possibly do without growing a second pair of hands?"

Shayla began slowly. "You might have heard that

Detective Gabriel Cortland has recently joined the homicide division."

"I have minions who tell me things, yes," Valri responded. Even as she talked, she seemed to be going full speed ahead at her keyboard, her fingers flying. "What about him?"

"Well, he's very closemouthed," Shayla continued, trying to find the right way to word her request.

"Heard that, too," Valri confirmed. Making a notation for herself, she moved her chair slightly and switched to another screen. That was when Shayla realized that the woman was working two monitors at the same time. She began to talk faster.

"Well, the chief of d's partnered us up," Shayla told Valri.

The latter flashed a smile at her.

"At your request, wasn't it?" It wasn't really a question, but Valri was curious to see what the family's newest detective would have to say about that.

"Yes." Shayla quickly launched into an explanation. "Detective Gabriel Cortland has the saddest eyes I've ever seen. I thought that maybe, if I was partnered with him, I could find a way to bring him around, help him rise above that sadness."

"Very noble. And how do I fit into this, since you're obviously here because you need something from me?" Valri concluded.

"I need to know *why* Cortland is so sad. It's nothing that he said—heaven knows the man doesn't talk," she told her cousin. "It's just the look in his eyes that gets to me." She lowered her voice so that it wouldn't carry to the other computer techs who worked under Valri. "I thought that maybe there's something in his personal records that would give me a clue, point me in the right direction." Shayla looked hopefully at her extremely proficient cousin.

Valri's expression didn't change. "In other words, you're hoping I would breach his privacy to satisfy your curiosity?" she guessed.

"It's not curiosity," Shayla told her. "I can't help him if I don't know why he's the way he is."

"Why don't you try asking him?" Valri suggested.

Shayla gave the computer expert a look. "If it was that simple, I would have already done it. The man is more closemouthed than a clam whose top and bottom were sealed together with crazy glue. I can barely pry 'hello' out of him. Predominantly, he speaks in grunts. I need help here. Specifically—" she looked at Valri pointedly "—I need *your* help."

Valri frowned slightly, looking at the various piles of folders on her extra-wide desk, all of which corresponded to different requests she had received. Gesturing at the stacks of folders, she said, "I have all these requests ahead of you. I haven't seen the bottom of my desk in months. Maybe even years," she added wistfully.

"I just need a hint, Valri. Something, *anything*, to get me moving in the right direction. I have this really uneasy feeling that the man is going to implode if I don't find a way to help him," she confided, leaning over Valri's desk again. "The man hardly eats, doesn't sleep much. I practically had to force-feed him a steak sandwich from Malone's."

"He is bad off, isn't he?" Valri commented. "The steak sandwiches from Malone's are my idea of heaven.

"I won't ask how you know he doesn't sleep much," Valri continued. "Okay, take a seat over there and give me a few minutes. I won't be able to give you much, but I can gather the basic headlines, and then you can take it from there. How's that?"

"That's terrific! I'm really grateful to you, Valri," Shayla told her cousin with feeling.

"Yeah, yeah. Go. Sit," she ordered, pointing toward a chair that was some distance away from hers.

Shayla did as she was told, crossing her fingers as she walked away. If anyone could help shed light on the situation, it was Valri.

Chapter 7

Shayla was prepared to settle in and wait for a while in order to get some sort of an answer. She realized that she was interrupting Valri, and whatever the computer expert came up with, she would gladly run with it, because, right now, she had nothing.

To her surprise, she didn't have to wait all that long. She barely had time to sit back in the chair before she saw Valri's body language become rigid as her eyes scanned the screen before her.

A moment later, the computer wizard looked up and was beckoning to her to come over.

Extremely hopeful, Shayla didn't even remember crossing the floor back to her cousin's desk. However, her eagerness was tempered with a note of caution. *That* was coupled with an underlying feeling of dread. If anyone had asked her why she felt that way, she wouldn't have been able to explain the origin of the sensation in the pit of her stomach—she just knew that it was there.

"What did you find?" Shayla asked, still attempting to interrupt the expression on the computer expert's face.

Valri glanced toward her cousin, then back at the screen she had just pulled up. "You do know that Cortland had been tracking the LA Moonlight Killer, right?" she asked. When Shayla nodded, the computer expert continued, "Cortland transferred here when it looked as if the killer was taking his spree away from LA."

"Yes, I know," Shayla said.

Valri measured her next words carefully. "Did you also know that, when Cortland was getting too close, the Moonlight Killer killed Cortland's wife?"

Shayla didn't remember sitting down in the chair next to Valri's desk, but she must have, because she found herself there when her knees suddenly gave way.

"No," she whispered in a horrified voice, "I didn't know that."

But Valri wasn't finished giving her all the heart-wrenching details yet. "His *pregnant* wife," the computer expert emphasized.

Shayla's hands flew to her mouth to keep the cry of horror back. She could almost feel her scream ricocheting in her throat. The information made her sick to her stomach.

Her eyes filled with tears, but she managed to keep them from spilling out.

"Oh, how awful for him," Shayla cried. It all made

sense to her now. She could totally understand why Cortland was so obsessed with catching this particular killer. And why there was so much sadness about the man.

Valri looked up from the screen she had been scrolling. "It looks like this killer is obsessed with your Detective Cortland," she commented to her cousin.

Shayla was about to correct her cousin that Cortland wasn't *her* detective, but since she was partnered with the man, it might sound like she was just splitting hairs, she thought. What really mattered here was that Cortland had lost his wife to this maniac. He was going to need help in tracking down this serial killer and bringing him in.

Shayla swallowed, trying to keep her breakfast down. The details Valri had just given her made that a challenge.

"Anything else?" she asked, doing her best to come around.

"Isn't that enough?" Valri asked her in surprise.

"Yes, it is," Shayla acknowledged sadly. "I just wanted to know if the report contained any other bombshells I should know about."

Valri looked back at the report on her monitor. "Only that when his wife was killed—he discovered the body, by the way," she added as a potent footnote, "Cortland went on an extensive bender that all but killed him. Because he had been such an exemplary detective and this crime was such an unspeakably horrific blow to him, his superiors tried to look the other way," she told her cousin as she quickly scanned the information. "Luckily, Cortland eventually cleaned up his act and asked to be transferred. I gather that his sole purpose in life became finding the killer and, I'm assuming, bringing him to justice."

Finished with her update, Valri sighed as she looked at Shayla. "I certainly don't envy you, Shay," she said, thinking about her cousin leaving here and trying to deal with her partner armed with this information.

"That makes two of us," Shayla murmured.

Valri's curiosity got the better of her. "So what are you going to do?" she asked. "Ask for another partner?"

Shayla's eyes met her cousin's. Valri knew better than that, she thought. "No way on earth," she told her cousin firmly.

Valri laughed softly. "I didn't think so," she replied. "Let me know if there's anything else I can do to help."

Shayla barely heard her. Nodding, she murmured, "Will do," as she quickly left the computer lab.

That poor man, Shayla couldn't help thinking as she hurried to the elevator. What Valri had told her kept replaying in her head. Fighting back tears again, Shayla tried to picture herself in his place, coming home and discovering the murdered body of his wife. It was just too awful to contemplate.

No wonder he had trouble sleeping. She wouldn't have been able to close her eyes in his place, not without being haunted by visions of what he had seen.

Impatience overwhelmed her. She had no idea how she was going to handle the situation once she was in the same room with Cortland. The main thing she had to remember was to curb her desire to throw her arms around the man and just hug him in an attempt to comfort her partner.

That was the way things were done in her family, but Shayla knew Cortland wouldn't appreciate that. The detective would most likely view it as a display of pity on her part rather than having her really feeling for him.

Well, she would find some way of comforting the man, she promised herself. To assist him with his mission—because that's what it was—and help him eventually come back to the living.

She knew now what she was up against. Armed with this information, she needed to get on with what needed to be done and, along the way, help Cortland take possession of his soul again.

He couldn't be allowed to let despair overwhelm him.

Determined, Shayla got off on her floor. It took her a second to hear the sobbing.

Heart-wrenching sobbing.

The sound was coming from a young woman one of the uniformed officers was attempting to talk to. He was also trying to quiet her down.

The officer was failing.

Shayla quickened her pace and walked up to the unusual pair. When she drew closer, she realized that the officer was trying to bring the young woman into the homicide squad room. The distraught young woman didn't even seem to hear him. Or, if she did, she wasn't processing what he was saying to her.

The moment that Shayla walked up, the officer's eyes darted in her direction, and he looked incredibly relieved.

For her part, Shayla looked from the police officer to the distraught young woman he was unsuccessfully trying to calm down.

"Can I help you?" Shayla asked the officer.

The story instantly came pouring out. "I found her like this downstairs, Detective. Every time I asked her what was wrong, she choked up and couldn't answer me. She just kept crying." The look on the young officer's face said that he realized his narrative was disjointed. He tried to explain his reasoning. "I saw a trace of blood on her shirt and thought maybe I should bring her up to Homicide."

The shell-shocked brunette's eyes widened a little at the mention of the word *homicide*, but she still didn't say anything. She just kept on sobbing.

The officer mutely appealed to Shayla for help. "I'm already late for my shift," he told her.

She knew what was probably coming. He was going to ask her for help. Given the situation, she felt she couldn't refuse. "I'll take it from here, Officer—"

She looked at the policeman, waiting for a name.

The man finally came to. "Yates," he said, raising his voice to be heard above the sobbing woman. "Ron Yates."

Shayla made a mental note of the officer's name in case she had more questions for him later.

"I'll get in contact if there's anything to tell you," she promised, then turned her attention toward the woman. "Why don't you come in with me so you can sit down?" she suggested kindly. "And then you can tell me just what happened."

"I don't know," the woman gasped, her voice cracking.

They were the first words the woman had offered, and Shayla seized them immediately. "Maybe if we start at the beginning," she coaxed, taking the sobbing woman by the hand and slowly leading her into the squad room.

Everyone in the front of the squad room turned to look at them, especially when the young woman finally managed to choke out an attention-getting phrase. "She's dead!"

And just like that, the room was alive with detectives and police personnel, all converging around Shayla and the sobbing woman with her.

Doing her best to focus on the distraught brunette, Shayla led her to her desk and had the woman sit down in the chair that faced hers.

Shayla noted that Cortland had drawn closer as well.

"What happened?" Cortland asked his partner before anyone else had a chance to voice the question.

"I haven't been able to get that out of her yet," Shayla told him honestly. "Maybe you'll have better luck."

The commotion had succeeded in drawing Hollandale out of his office as well. He immediately made his way over to Shayla's desk. The other detectives drew back, giving the lieutenant space.

"What's going on here?" he asked, his eyes sweeping over the scene.

"Officer Yates brought her up here," Shayla explained. "He said he found her like this. He couldn't get her to talk, but he saw the blood on her clothes, so he thought that she might have either witnessed a homicide or been part of one," she guess, filling in the details into Yates's anemic narrative for the lieutenant's benefit as well as Cortland's.

Hollandale nodded. He had learned to roll with the punches a long time ago.

"Why don't you come into my office, ma'am?" he politely requested, making it seem that the choice was hers to make instead of his.

The woman rubbed the heel of her hand against her tearstained face, trying to dry it.

"Cavanaugh, since you brought her in, why don't you come along, too?" Hollandale suggested. He began to turn, then paused. His eyes swept over her partner. "Cortland?"

It was all he said and all that he really needed to say.

The dark-haired detective followed in their wake.

Like a deflated balloon, the sobbing woman collapsed into a chair the moment the lieutenant directed her toward it.

"Would you like something to drink?" Hollandale asked the woman. "Water? Coffee? Soda?"

She shook her head in response to each suggestion. Instead, she pressed her hands against her lips as if attempting to pull herself together so that she could finally say some intelligible words.

Shayla moved closer to the woman. Ever so gently, she took the woman's hands into her own. "Take your time," she told her. "I'm Detective Shayla Cavanaugh. This is Detective Cortland, and this is our commander, Lieutenant Hollandale." She looked at the woman, who was marginally beginning to settle down. "When you're ready, you can tell us your name."

"Maureen," the brunette finally said. "Maureen O'Hara." A knowing half smile quirked her mouth. "My mother loved old movies," she explained. Her voice broke just then, and she struggled to continue.

"Take your time, Ms. O'Hara," the lieutenant advised gently.

Maureen raised her head, still struggling to contain her emotions. After a moment, she began talking again, although it was obvious difficult for her to keep her voice steady.

"I came in early to get my check. The door wasn't locked, but—" Her voice broke again, and she pressed her lips together.

"But what?" Hollandale asked kindly.

Shayla noticed that Cortland hadn't said a word since he came in with them. Instead, he was watching the young woman intently, like he was waiting for something to rise to the forefront.

"But it didn't look like there was anyone there," she said helplessly. "At first," she added belatedly. Fresh tears rose to her eyes.

"Where do you work, Maureen?" Shayla asked the young woman.

"It's a twenty-four-hour convenience store on Alton and Yale," the woman said, studying her fingertips as if the answer was somehow found there. "It wasn't my shift, but I wanted to get my check, so…so I stopped by and…and…that's when I saw her," she sobbed, her voice breaking.

"Saw who?" The deep voice startled them. All three people in the room turned to look at Cortland, who had finally spoken up.

"Shirley." There was almost a look of agony in the young woman's eyes as she answered the question.

"Shirley?" Cortland repeated.

"I don't know her last name," Maureen lamented. "I should, but I don't. Didn't," she corrected herself, as if that information existed in the past but no longer in the present.

"Where was Shirley?" Shayla asked. She was aware that the lieutenant was observing both her and Cortland, undoubtedly wanting to see how they performed under strained circumstances, she thought.

"On the floor," Maureen answered, her voice cracking. "She was all tied up in this awful, bizarre way. There was a thin rope around one of her ankles, and it led up to her throat. It looked as if she had choked herself, but that doesn't make any sense." Maureen looked at Hollandale. "Does it?"

There were details that had been left out of news reports on the serial killer's murders. The detectives who had been involved in trying to catch the killer were aware of them, but the public had been kept in the dark about the killer's very strange way of tying up his victims that brought about their demise.

"Anything else?" Hollandale gently coaxed.

The young woman looked down at the blood on her sleeve.

"Yeah," she answered, her voice hollow, as if she was trying to separate herself from the image that hovered in her mind's eye. "There was blood on her left cheek, and it looked like someone had—had—" She covered her face with her hands, as if that could somehow wipe away the image she saw—but it couldn't.

"Had carved initials into her face," Cortland filled in.

The woman looked at him, stricken. "Yes!" she cried then began sobbing again.

Chapter 8

It wasn't easy, not to mention somewhat time-consuming, but by speaking slowly and calmly to the distraught young woman, Shayla and Lieutenant Hollandale eventually managed to piece together the choppy information Maureen gave them.

They found out that the traumatized clerk had practically tripped over the other woman's body. Horrified, rather than calling the police, Maureen had run out of the store and away from the crime scene.

The details were all jumbled up as they emerged from her mouth. She didn't even seem to know how long it had taken her to get from the convenience store to the precinct, but somehow, she had eventually managed to stumble into the police station.

That was where, Shayla told the other two men, Officer Yates had found her. Listening, Hollandale nodded. He looked far from pleased. "Looks like that LA serial killer did resurface here after all." The lieutenant looked at the two detectives in his office. "Cortland, Cavanaugh, take a couple of uniforms with you, call in a CSI team and head over to the crime scene."

Maureen looked horrified at this turn of events. Her eyes darted from the detectives to the lieutenant. "Please don't make me go back there!" she begged as she began to shake.

"Don't worry about that," the lieutenant told her in a comforting tone. "Right now, all we need from you is the address of the convenience store. We would like you to stay here and give your statement to Detective Lorenzo."

Maureen nodded numbly. A small woman, she looked as if she wanted to fold up into herself if she possibly could.

"The store is on the corner of Alton and Yale," she said, her voice cracking.

The lieutenant called in two uniformed officers. He gave the two policemen the address.

Meanwhile, Shayla was calling the CSI division, requesting that a team, along with an accompanying coroner, be sent to the scene of the crime.

It was all attended to in record time.

"Shouldn't you wait until you're sure that there *is* a crime scene?" Gabriel asked her as they took the stairs out of the building and headed to the parking lot.

"Did she sound as if she was making all this up to you?" Shayla asked in surprise.

Gabriel shrugged. He'd had time to think, and he realized that hoping the serial killer would materialize might have colored the way he viewed everything. Maybe it made him believe the young woman's story when he should have held it somewhat suspect.

"People lie about all sorts of things for all sorts of reasons," Gabriel told her.

"Maybe," Shayla allowed. "But Maureen looked too sick to her stomach to be making all this up. And if we wait to verify the information before calling in CSI, that's that much more time that we've managed to lose. We've already lost more time than we should have."

Reaching the bottom of the stairs, she looked at Cortland. She was determined to have him think of her as his partner, not a cross he had to bear. Which was why she asked him, "You want to take your car or mine to the crime scene?"

Cortland didn't hesitate for a second. "Mine."

Shayla smiled to herself. She thought so. Cortland struck her as someone who needed to be in control at all times. Given what Valri had told her, she saw no reason for her to point out the obvious to her partner—that she was far more familiar with the area than he was. If he wanted to drive, then so be it.

Turning on her heel, Shayla made her way over toward where his vehicle was parked. Standing next to it, she surprised Cortland.

He scowled at her, confused. "How did you know which one was mine?"

"I like being prepared," she told him cheerfully. "That car was parked in the space that corresponded to your apartment number when I came by last night to bring you the sandwich and fries."

That gave him pause for a moment. "All right," he said, hitting the button on his key fob that opened all the locks on his vehicle.

Getting in, he looked at the GPS on his dashboard. He didn't want to admit that he needed help, but he knew he had to. It was either that or waste time driving around in circles. "What did you say the address of this convenience store was?" he asked.

Rather than tell him, Shayla leaned over and typed in the address on his GPS. Finished, she smiled at him. "There."

"Thanks," Gabriel bit off. Putting the car in gear, he took off.

The two uniform policemen had gotten to the destination a couple of beats ahead of them. Drawing closer, Gabriel saw that telltale yellow crime scene tape stretched across the store's doorway. A very small crowd had begun to gather outside, speculating on what had happened.

Shayla wove her way through the small crowd, ignoring their questions for the time being. Cortland walked ahead of her, forging a path for both of them.

Walking into the convenience store, Shayla saw the victim lying on the floor behind the counter. The woman was tied up the way Maureen had described.

Shayla instantly looked up at Cortland for his reaction. In her opinion, her partner looked numb and pale.

"Are you all right?" she whispered to Cortland.

"Yeah," he snapped, then looked at her accusingly. "Why shouldn't I be?"

"No reason," she answered, attempting to brush the whole thing off.

But it wasn't in her to lie. Being part of a police-oriented family had its consequences. One of which was to always tell the truth, no matter what.

So she did.

"I just thought it might bring up some bad memories," she admitted.

Was she implying something, he couldn't help wondering, growing defensive. "There are no good memories when it comes to homicide," he informed her coldly.

"No, there aren't," Shayla readily agreed. Taking out her cell phone, she bent close to the victim and snapped a few photographs.

"I thought CSI did that sort of thing," Gabriel said, surprised to see that this woman he had to put up with was taking pictures of the grim scene.

"Oh, they do," she assured him. "I just like to have my own set. Maybe I can see something in the ones I take that aren't visible in the other photos," she explained.

Crouching next to the victim, Shayla could feel her heart aching. "Poor thing never had a chance," she murmured. She looked the dead woman over carefully. "I think the killer took her completely by surprise. There aren't even any defensive wounds on her. She didn't have a chance to fight back." Shayla could feel a chill slithering down her spine. "This guy's a sick monster."

"Well, we agree on that," Cortland told her.

He slowly surveyed the entirety of the small, crowded crime scene. Unlike some convenience stores that had several aisles customers could wander down, this store was relatively small, crowded with displays that took up almost all the available space.

"We're not dealing with a big guy," Shayla concluded.

"What makes you say that?" Cortland asked, curious as to the thought process that led her to this conclusion.

"Nothing's knocked over," she pointed out. "If the killer was a big man, in a place like this, all sorts of things would have been toppled over."

She looked at the woman on the floor again. She wished the coroner would arrive so those awful ropes could be taken off the victim. They were dehumanizing.

"The second he put his hands on her," Shayla continued, "she would have tried to run away."

"Not necessarily," Cortland told her, circling the woman's body like a bloodhound that had caught the scent of something and was now zeroing in on it.

"Are you saying he charmed her?" Shayla asked, trying to follow Cortland's thinking.

"No," he answered, still circling the inert body, "I'm saying that he gave her a shot of something that immobilized her, knocked her out so that he could tie her up like some lassoed rodeo calf. Probably walked up behind her like he was going to ask her a question, then injected her." He had his guess as to what the killer might have used.

She looked at Cortland, horror stricken. "I hadn't thought of that."

"I did," Gabriel answered grimly.

Moved, thinking of what he had to have gone through, finding his wife this way, before she could stop herself, Shayla said, "I'm sorry."

Gabriel thought she was referring to what the victim had gone through before she died and allowed himself a moment to feel sorry for the murdered woman.

"Yeah," he replied, looking at the dead woman. "Me, too."

Shayla read what the detective was thinking in his face. She was about to correct him, then decided that it was better this way. He wouldn't suddenly turn defensive on her, and she wouldn't have to admit that she knew about what had happened to his wife. She thought it would be better if she was more prepared to voice the right sentiments in the right way. She didn't want to give the detective cause to snarl at her.

The next moment, she heard her uncle's deep voice.

"I'm not sure we're all going to be able to fit in here," Sean Cavanaugh said as he arrived at the convenience store with his team in tow. He paused just inside the doorway with its yellow tape. "I'm not even sure there's enough room for our equipment." Sean nodded at the new detective he didn't recognize and then smiled at his niece. "What do you have for me?"

"Apparently the Moonlight Killer's latest victim, I think," she told her uncle when Cortland made no response to her question.

"The Moonlight Killer?" the CSI leader repeated,

somewhat taken aback. "It's been over nine months since anyone's heard from that creep. I was hoping that, if nothing else, maybe he had retired. Or died."

"Not hardly," Gabriel replied, rocking back on his heels.

Shayla had noticed that her partner had been combing through the various debris on the floor, obviously searching for something.

From the look on Cortland's face, Shayla judged, he had just found it.

"What do you have?" she asked, nodding at his hand. His glove-covered fingers were curled around something.

"A broken syringe." The item was lying in the center of his blue-gloved hand.

"You were right," Shayla cried excitedly, standing on her toes and peering over Cortland's broad shoulder.

"Of course I was right," he answered.

"Would either of you want to let me in on what you're talking about?" Sean asked.

Rather than speak up the way Gabriel assumed that his partner would, Shayla took a step back and gestured toward him, giving him the floor.

"Go ahead," she said. "You're a lot more familiar with the way this sick SOB operates than I am."

Cortland's face was grim as he slowly described how the Moonlight Killer managed to get the drop on the women he singled out to be his victims. "It looks like he manages to come up behind them and injects them with some sort of a neuromuscular blocking agent."

Sean looked surprised, then nodded. "I'm familiar

with that substance. It's fast acting and immobilizes the victim so that they can't move, can't speak, but they're not unconscious. They're aware of everything that's going on around them. I once heard of couples supposedly using it to enhance the whole sexual experience, but that's just a line of bull," Sean concluded. "It's an awful way to victimize someone."

"That's not available to just anyone, is it?" Shayla asked her uncle.

"No, a person would have to be a doctor to get their hands on it. It's meant as a fallback during surgery," Sean told her.

"A doctor or some kind of other medical professional," Shayla expanded, thinking out loud. "Like a nurse practitioner. Or maybe a pharmacist," she guessed.

"All possibilities," Sean agreed. He snapped out of his thoughts. "Well, I've got a crime scene to process," he told the duo, excusing himself.

Shayla moved out of her uncle's way and looked at her partner. He was looking particularly grim at the moment. "Are you all right?" she asked.

Irritated, he almost snapped at her. If they had been alone, he would have. "Why do you keep asking me that?" he demanded.

"You look pale," she explained. "I would have thought that by now, you would have reached a saturation point with these murders."

He shrugged. "No more than anyone else dealing with homicides," he said. And then he looked at her more closely. "There's something else, isn't there?"

There was, but she didn't think now was a good time to broach it. Maybe when he had gotten to know her better—and trusted her more—she could tell him what she had found out. "Why don't we question some of the people in the area, find out if they might have seen something last night, instead of quizzing each other?" she suggested brightly.

He gestured for her to lead the way, but he wasn't convinced that there wasn't something she wasn't telling him—something she was holding back.

They combed the area, but after canvassing the nearby stores, all of which had been closed at the time the murder had taken place, they weren't able to find anyone who could tell them anything had might shed any light on the circumstances.

As they made their way back toward the convenience store, Shayla noticed a restaurant across the way. She pointed it out.

"It has a surveillance camera outside the window that might have picked up something," she suggested to her partner, "but I wouldn't get my hopes up."

"I'm not," he told her.

As it turned out, she was right. The camera was broken and had been left up to hopefully deter robberies until it was fixed, the embarrassed restaurant owner explained.

After several hours of canvassing the local stores in the area, they had nothing to show for their trouble. None of the surveillance cameras—the working ones— had captured anything worthwhile.

The Moonlight Killer, Shayla thought, remained as big a mystery now as he had been before the convenience store worker had lost her life.

It felt like forever before they finally returned to Cortland's vehicle and got in.

He glanced in Shayla's direction as he buckled up. "You look drained," Cortland commented.

"I am," she said, sighing. "This is my first serial killer. How do you do it?"

Cortland started up the Crown Victoria. He had no idea what she was talking about. "How do I do what?"

"How do you manage to keep going?" she asked Cortland.

He didn't answer immediately. Instead, he waited until he could stop at a light, and then he looked at her. He understood where she was going with this now.

"Because throwing up my hands is not going to capture this SOB and get those women the justice that they all deserve," he told her. He tossed her another pointed glance before continuing to drive back to the precinct. "Anything else?" he asked.

"No," she answered quietly. "Not right now."

Chapter 9

When they walked into the homicide squad room, Shayla and her partner went to see their lieutenant. She assumed Cortland would be the one to describe the crime scene to their superior. But he sat down in front of Hollandale's desk, remaining silent, so she was forced to start talking, giving Hollandale a summary of what they had seen and dealt with.

Finished, Shayla slid forward to the edge of her seat and asked the lieutenant, "Do you think that there is any way you could put pressure on whatever coroner is on duty today to do the autopsy on the convenience store victim first? Or at least complete that autopsy before the end of day?"

The lieutenant looked at both of the detectives. "Is there some question about the way the woman was killed?" Hollandale asked. From the input he had already received, the cause of death seemed pretty cut-and-dried.

It was on the tip of Shayla's tongue to tell the lieutenant about Cortland's theory regarding the drug that may have been used to render the poor woman immobile. But that information belonged to her partner.

She forced herself to look at the detective sitting next to her. "Cortland found something," she told the lieutenant.

Hollandale turned his chair slightly to face the silent detective. "I'm listening, Cortland," he said, waiting for the man to start talking.

Gabriel preferred *doing* to *talking*, but it was obvious to him that he had no choice, so he told his superior, "I think the killer uses a neuromuscular blocking agent to render his victims immobile before he ties them up." Each word cost him, and he tried not to think about Natalie suffering at this maniac's hands.

"You think?" the lieutenant asked, clearly asking for some sort of proof to back up this theory.

Gabriel frowned. He wasn't keen on performing like some sort of trained seal, but he also knew he couldn't go on operating on his own. Everyone in this precinct supported teamwork. If this serial killer was going to be caught, he needed to accept that fact and be part of that team.

"I know," Gabriel corrected himself, enunciating the two words in a clear, firm voice for the lieutenant's benefit.

Seeing her partner's discomfort, Shayla immediately jumped in. "That's why we need that autopsy done as soon as possible," she explained. "So we can get a clearer picture of what we're dealing with."

Hollandale nodded agreeably. "If the coroner on duty is swamped for some reason, I'll see if I can get another set of hands down there to handle the clerk's autopsy," he promised, then asked, "Did any of the locals see anything that might prove useful?"

Shayla shook her head. "No one was even out walking their dog when this happened," she answered. "Cortland and I went around the neighborhood, but it was mostly stores and restaurants, all of which were closed for the night at that time."

She knew what the lieutenant's next question was going to be and beat him to it. "There weren't very many surveillance cameras in the area, either, and the ones that were there either weren't working, or, according to the store owner, hadn't recorded anything."

The lieutenant turned toward the newest detective to join the squad. "Anything to add, Cortland?"

"No, Cavanaugh covered everything, sir," Gabriel told his superior respectfully.

"From what I'm told," Hollandale said with a smile, glancing toward Shayla, "she usually does." The lieutenant moved forward in his chair. "All right, write up your reports and see if you can come up with any connections to the other victims who were killed by this psychopath. We still don't know what makes him single out the women he kills."

Shayla rose to her feet, as did Cortland. "Yes, sir,"

she said, answering for both of them. "You will be the first to know if we find a pattern."

Gabriel expected her to say something about the meeting, but she didn't. Instead, she hurried back to her desk. The moment she got there, Shayla sat down and picked up the telephone receiver.

Normally, curiosity was something Gabriel could easily contain and ignore unless it was directly related to a case he was working on, at which point he would explore—on his own—whatever it was that had aroused his curiosity in the first place.

But this woman he had been forced to work with had somehow managed to affect his usual way of thinking and had spurred his curiosity.

Gabriel heard himself asking her, "Who are you calling?"

About to answer him, Shayla was forced to hold up her hand like a traffic cop, telling him to hold on to that thought as she heard the receiver on the other end being picked up.

"Kristin, hi, it's Shayla. Christian's sister," she added since there were so many family members floating around, sometimes it was hard putting a face to a name. Now that she had the lieutenant's blessing, she wanted to get this autopsy moving along as quickly as possible. "I need a favor—it's sanctioned by my lieutenant, in case you're wondering. Lieutenant Hollandale," she supplied, adding, "He's the new man in charge of the homicide division."

Shayla heard the medical examiner pause for a moment, as if she was thinking, then say, "I'm familiar with him. What do you—and he—need?" Kristin asked.

"We need an autopsy done on this convenience store clerk who was found dead this morning, and we need the report as soon as possible." In case the medical examiner had misgivings, Shayla added, "Apparently, the Moonlight Killer has moved his base of operation from LA to our fair little city."

"Oh Lord, we didn't need this." Kristin sighed. "Is there anything in particular that you are looking for or hoping to find in this report?"

Shayla give her a quick summation. "My partner found a syringe near the victim's body. He believes that the killer injected his victim with a neuromuscular blocking agent in order to paralyze her. If you can find any indication of that in her system, it might help us narrow our list of people to look at and consider."

"Because not everyone can get their hands on this drug," Kristin guessed.

"Exactly. So, do you think you'll be able to get down to the morgue?" she asked hopefully.

"I need to make a phone call first," the medical examiner told the young woman she had inherited the day that she had married Malloy Cavanaugh, "but yes, I can get down to the morgue. Nothing I like doing better on my day off than an autopsy," she told Shayla with a laugh.

Shayla breathed a sigh of relief. "Thank you, Kris. I owe you."

"Yes," Kristin agreed. "You do. And I plan to collect on that promise when I find myself needing a baby-sitter."

Shayla nearly dropped the receiver. "You don't mean for Malloy, do you?" she asked.

"Nope," Kristin answered.

Shayla could practically hear the grin in her cousin-in-law's voice. Malloy had to be pleased as anything, she thought, herself immensely delighted. "When?"

"Seven months from now. You have time," Kristin told her.

"I think that's wonderful! Keep me posted," she said.

Kristin laughed. "I plan to keep everyone posted. As for your other request, I'll be at the morgue as soon as possible."

"Are you sure you can handle it?" she asked, concerned now that this newest piece of information had come up.

"Hey, I'm a Cavanaugh," Kristin reminded her. "Even if it is by marriage. We Cavanaughs can handle everything—or so it said on my wedding certificate. See you," she said just before she hung up.

Shayla could almost feel Cortland's eyes on her the entire time she had been on the phone. The moment she put down the receiver, he asked, "What was that all about?"

"We have a medical examiner in the family," she told her partner. "I just got her to agree to come in on her day off to do our victim's autopsy. Otherwise, we might have to wait until sometime tomorrow or even the day after that to find out if that immobilizing drug you mentioned was in her system. From what I gather," she went on, "there are a number of autopsies at the morgue waiting to be done ahead of our victim's."

But that wasn't what he was asking about. "Do you always squeal gleefully when arranging for an autopsy?"

She had forgotten about that, Shayla thought. She hadn't meant to let that sound slip. Gabriel was obviously waiting for an answer.

"No, that was personal," she said, hoping that was enough to satisfy him. It wasn't. She sighed, continuing. "The medical examiner, Kristin Alberghetti Cavanaugh, is married to my cousin Malloy Cavanaugh."

It still wasn't making any sense to him. "Is that why you squealed?"

To be honest, Gabriel didn't even know why he was asking. But since he had gotten stuck in this work relationship, he felt that he might as well try to make it work. Or at least understand it—and her.

Who knew, her answer might even turn out to be useful to him down the line, although he did have his doubts. So far, working with this woman who had relatives hiding in every nook and cranny at the precinct was one great big chaotic mystery—not to mention a pain.

"No," she answered, searching madly for a reason to give him to explain why she had suddenly sounded so joyous. Normally, she would have had no problem telling him—or anyone—the real reason. This pregnancy was just wonderful news.

But in this case, it would just unearth some terrible memories and subject Cortland to a great deal of pain. Pain she didn't want him experiencing.

"So why did you squeal?" Gabriel asked.

Shayla pressed her lips together. If Cortland did stay in the homicide division for a while, he was bound to see Kristin's condition for himself. He might as well hear it from her now.

"I just found out that my cousin's wife is pregnant," she told Gabriel. Shayla never took her eyes off her partner's face.

A whole barrage of emotions passed through him before Gabriel was able to completely shut down his expression and get hold of his thoughts.

Shayla could see the man's pain, and for the second time since she had found out about his wife, she felt that overwhelming desire to comfort him, to somehow attempt to take away at least some of the pain that Cortland had to be feeling.

"I'm sorry," Shayla said as she put her hand on his shoulder.

Gabriel shrugged it off. Not trusting himself to speak, he strode toward the doorway and crossed the threshold, going out into the hall.

For half a second, Shayla thought of just letting him go. But she had never been one to step away and hope that things would just take care of themselves. She knew that wasn't the way things were done.

So instead of watching her partner go, she was on her feet, moving fast and hoping to catch up with Gabriel before he disappeared.

She managed to reach him just as he was about to open the door to the stairway. Well, at least he hadn't disappeared into the elevator.

"Wait," she implored, making a grab for his shoulder.

Unlike in the office, this was not a hand on his shoulder that was meant to offer comfort. What she was trying to do was to hold her partner in place until she could get the man to listen to her.

Gabe knew he could very easily shake her off and keep going until he could get hold of himself. But instead, he just looked at her, waiting for some sort of an explanation and trying his damnedest to get hold of his rampaging emotions.

"What?" he demanded.

There was no way around this. She had to tell him and fervently hope that instead of shutting off communication between them altogether, it would somehow magically open it up.

"I know," she told him, lowering her voice at the last second as someone walked by. Shayla didn't want the woman in the hall to hear what she was about to say.

He waited until the person passed. "Know what?" he all but growled.

She never took her eyes off his. "I know about your wife."

His first instinct was to pull away and storm off. But instead, Gabriel forced himself to say, between clenched teeth, "Know what?"

"That she was a victim of the LA Moonlight Killer," Shayla answered. They were not the easiest words to for her to utter, especially since she was still looking her partner in the eye. But she felt that looking away would have somehow been insulting to the memory of the woman he had lost. "I am so sorry," she told him

again, unable to find another way to offer him her con-
dolences or to comfort her partner.

She had learned a long time ago that everyone who
had ever lost a loved one had to find their own way
back. The only thing she could do was offer her presence to him whenever he felt like talking about what he
was going through—if he ever even got to that point.

"Yeah," Gabriel bit off dismissively. And then he
suddenly looked up at her. He had a feeling that wasn't
all. "What else do you know?" he asked, pinning her
in place.

This was even more difficult to say than the first
part had been, she thought. She debated pretending that
there wasn't anything else, but she had a feeling that
Cortland wouldn't be so easily led astray. With all her
heart, she wished she had made her call to Kristin in
private so that none of this would be coming to light
anywhere around her partner right now.

Shayla forced the words out. "I know that your wife
was pregnant at the time the serial killer snuffed out
her life."

"She wasn't a candle," Gabriel shouted at her before
he could get hold of himself.

None of this was coming out the way she wanted it
to. "I didn't mean to imply that she was. I'm trying to
apologize here, Gabriel," she explained, then added, "I
don't usually walk into something that I need to apologize for. I'm usually the one who says the right thing
at the right time, even when everyone else is at a loss
for words." She blew out a breath, wondering if there

was anything else she could possibly say to somehow make up for the fact that she had walked right into this.

He knew she meant well and that she was trying her best to say the right thing. But he just felt so angry about everything, including having his privacy invaded, that he couldn't immediately forgive Shayla.

Waving a dismissive hand at her, Gabriel told her, "Forget about it," in a detached, distant voice.

"I can't," Shayla told him honestly. "But now that it's out and you're aware of the fact that I know, I want *you* to know that if you ever need someone to talk to about what happened—or about anything at all, for that matter—I'm here for you. You can always talk to me if you need to."

He looked at her as if she had just told him that she intended to keep poking at the wound he'd suffered. All he wanted was for her to back off.

"I don't need or want to talk to anyone," he informed her pointedly. "Have I made myself clear?"

She wanted to argue with him about it, to tell him that no man was an island or could consider himself to be one.

Not even him.

But for now, she knew that the best thing she could do for her partner was back off and give him some time to heal—or at least go through the motions of attempting to heal.

"Perfectly." Regrouping, Shayla said, "All right, let's find a way to bring this killer in." With that, she turned on her heel and walked back to the squad room, hoping that he would decide to follow her.

After a couple of minutes, Cortland finally did.

Chapter 10

They were back the following day, working with the meager input they had gathered on the serial killer. As it turned out, Kristin had been unable to come in late yesterday, but she was in this morning and had called to tell them so.

Shayla noticed that Cortland kept checking his watch every so often. She knew he was waiting for Kristin to call back with information.

After observing his behavior several times, Shayla felt obligated to tell her partner, "Most autopsies take between two and four hours. Sometimes longer."

She was going to add that time didn't go by any faster if he kept looking at his watch, but she decided to keep that remark to herself.

Gabriel arched an eyebrow and gave her a look. "Your point?" he asked.

"No point," she answered innocently. "Just a fact that I wanted to throw out there." Because she felt her partner needed something concrete to hang on to, she went on to tell him, "Since we gave the medical examiner something specific to look for, she'll probably call us once the results of that test are in. Until then," she continued, looking down at her desk, "we've got all this paperwork to keep us busy." Leaning back in her chair, she blew out a breath. "And I don't know about you, but I feel like we're going around in circles."

Gabriel merely grunted. She took that as his way of agreeing.

They continued writing the reports and studying what they had managed to collect, which didn't amount to all that much. But in her opinion, "something" was always better than nothing.

After another hour had gone by, Shayla felt like everything was aching. She moved her neck back and forth, trying to get rid of the kink that seemed to have gathered at the very base and was now throbbing.

Closing her eyes, she took a minuscule break. A number of thoughts had been crowding in her brain. Opening her eyes again, she glanced at her partner. "You know, there's also the possibility that this wasn't the work of the Moonlight Killer at all."

Cortland eyed her sharply. "What do you mean?"

"Maybe she was killed by someone she knew, like an old boyfriend she had cheated on who was looking to get even with her and that's why there were no defensive wounds found on her. He caught her by surprise before she realized what he was up to and could fight back."

"You're forgetting about the syringe," Gabriel pointed out.

She *had* forgotten about that, Shayla realized. The way the clerk had been bound was also identical to the other victims, but the detail about the syringe had been left out of the other accounts, so only the killer and the LA police would know about that.

She hadn't known about that detail until Cortland had mentioned it.

"And you came across a syringe at one of the Moonlight Killer's murder scenes before?" she asked, just to be sure.

"Yes, I did," he answered flatly. His expression was dark.

She didn't have to ask her partner for further details. Instinctively, she knew that he'd probably found a syringe at the site of his wife's murder.

Shayla was about to go back to reviewing the files stacked on her desk for the umpteenth time when the phone next to her rang.

"Hopefully, that's the cavalry," she murmured, reaching for the receiver. "Cavanaugh."

"Shayla, can you and your partner get down here?" Kristin asked.

Up until the phone rang, she had felt as if she was in danger of having her eyes shutting on her. The moment she heard Kristin's voice on the other end of the line, Shayla felt as if she had suddenly come to life.

"Did you find something?" she asked, cradling the

phone against her neck and shoulder as she pulled her files together into one neat, orderly pile.

"I think so," Kristin answered, trying to keep the excitement out of her voice. "Since you gave me something specific to look for, I had the test identifying a neuromuscular blocking agent in her system fast-tracked. The results just came back a minute ago."

This could just lead them to the break that they were looking for, Shayla thought hopefully. At the very least, it was a start.

Pushing her chair away from her with the backs of her legs as she rose, Shayla told her cousin's wife, "We'll be right there."

Gabriel was on his feet immediately. "Your friend found something?" he asked. There was actually what passed for a hopeful note in his voice.

Shayla caught herself mentally crossing her fingers. "It sounds like it," she answered, already on her way into the hall.

Gabriel caught up to her in fewer than three strides and was ahead of her by the time he reached the elevator. Punching the down button, he looked over to the opposite wall at the door to the stairway when the elevator didn't immediately materialize.

It seemed as if he was planning on taking the stairs, Shayla thought.

"Why don't we just wait for the elevator?" she suggested. She wasn't in the mood to go dashing down the stairs unless it was absolutely unavoidable. "After all, you already know what the medical examiner is going to tell us." All the evidence pointed to the fact that Cortland was right about the drug in the victim's system.

"Maybe I like being validated," he answered in an offhanded manner. When his partner started laughing at his response, Cortland looked at her sharply. "What?"

"You are the very last person I would *ever* say actually needed to be validated," she told him. Just then, the elevator arrived and opened its doors.

She noticed that Gabriel looked relieved that there was no one else on it.

They got on quickly. Cortland jabbed the button for the basement as well as the one that closed the doors quickly. The elevator rumbled in response, then proceeded down to their destination.

"I'm not about to argue with you," Gabriel told her, referring to her comment about his not needing validation.

"Wait, let me mark that down," Shayla cried, pretending to make a notation of the date in the air. And then, thinking maybe she had gone a bit too far, she flashed an apologetic smile. "Sorry, most of the people I work with know when I'm kidding. And I kid a lot," she added. She looked at him to see his reaction. He still appeared rather solemn. "Kidding helps to relieve the tension. You should think about trying it sometime."

"Maybe later," he replied.

"Something to look forward to," Shayla said just as the elevator doors opened again.

Getting off, Cortland took a step toward the right.

"The morgue is in the other direction," Shayla told him as she began to walk toward the left. "It used to be located in another building that was off the premises, but they found that having the morgue in the same area where the CSI team did its research wound up saving time and effort," she explained.

Gabriel merely nodded and fell into step beside her. He discovered that he had to concentrate in order to keep from moving ahead of his partner.

As if reading his mind, Shayla told him, "In case you're wondering, I *am* walking fast." She punctuated her statement with a grin.

For a moment, she thought she caught a glimmer of a smile flicker in response to hers.

"Yeah," Gabriel answered. "I can tell."

Humor, wow, she thought. There was hope for the man after all.

"As long as you know," she said with as straight a face as she could manage. And then she grinned.

The hallway at this end of the basement broke into two different areas. The far larger area housed the crime scene investigators that her uncle Sean oversaw, while the much smaller area was reserved for the morgue, with its autopsy tables as well as the very deep drawers that housed bodies that were waiting either to be autopsied or to be moved to their final resting place. There was also the computer lab area which in essence was part of the Crime Scene Investigation department.

Walking into the morgue, the first person they encountered was Greg Allen, the medical examiner who was on duty for the day.

The person they were looking to speak to was all the way in the back of the room, dressed in her scrubs.

Much to her mother's everlasting disappointment, Dr. Kristin Cavanaugh had decided to give up her medical practice and become a medical examiner. She felt that she could do the most good in that capacity, speaking for the dead who were no longer able to speak for themselves.

"Kristin," Shayla called out as she and Gabriel walked in, "we got here as soon as we could." Reaching the medical examiner, Shayla paused. "You two haven't met yet, have you?" she realized. "This is my new partner, Detective Gabriel Cortland. Detective Cortland, this is Dr. Kristin Alberghetti Cavanaugh, the wonderful medical examiner who agreed to come in on one of her days off and fast-track this autopsy for us."

"Nice to meet you," Kristin said, nodding at Gabriel. "I'd shake hands, but…" Her voice trailed off as she held up her gloved hands.

Aware of the necessity to keep everything clean in the autopsy area, Gabriel returned the nod. "Same here. Thanks for coming in," he felt obligated to add.

"Shayla explained that you believed the victim was killed by the Moonlight Killer. I thought he only stalked his victims in LA," she commented as she led them back to the table where the latest victim had been autopsied and was now neatly sewn back together.

Gabriel tore his eyes away from the young woman's face. Despite the fact that she was partially draped with a sheet, seeing the convenience store victim like this just brought back too many vivid, painful memories of his wife.

Memories that had taken him a great many months to come to terms with.

Turning away from the victim, Gabriel looked at the medical examiner. "Did you find the neuromuscular blocking agent in her system?" he asked.

Kristin nodded. "She tested positive for the substance. How did you know?" she asked, looking from Gabriel to Shayla.

"The credit all belongs to Cortland," Shayla told her. "He was the one who saw the small puncture mark right behind her ear and found that near-empty syringe on the floor next to the victim." Because she thought that Kristin might need some further clarification, she added, "Cortland was also one of the detectives who had been working on the serial killer case back in LA."

Kristin nodded, thinking about what she had read about the case at the time. "I heard that there was a nine-month break in between LA's last case and now this one."

"There was," Gabriel answered grimly.

When he didn't say anything further, Kristin asked innocently, "Do we have any idea why that was?"

Shayla decided to step in, trying to save her partner from having to put up with any more questions at the moment.

"Just unproven speculation," she answered quickly. She saw the pile of pages lying on the side table. "Is that the autopsy report?" she asked the medical examiner hopefully.

"The unofficial one," Kristin answered. "It's not the formal version. That hasn't been finalized yet."

"Can we hang on to this until you've had a chance to write one up formally?" Gabriel asked, already reaching for the pages.

Kristin looked a little surprised at the request. "Sure, I guess," she answered.

"Right now," Shayla said to her cousin's wife, "since from all indications, the killer moved his base of operations from LA to Orange County—more specifically, to Aurora—it's like we've been moved back to square one. So far there are no eyewitnesses and no leads." She pointed to the pages that her partner was now holding in his hands. "This could very well wind up pointing us in the right direction to start our search."

Kristin smiled. "Well, after that sort of a buildup, how can I possibly say no?" she asked. "Sure. Take the preliminary report. I've got a copy of it. I can use it to extrapolate and further embellish on my findings. Do you want me to send that to you when I'm done?"

Shayla smiled warmly at the other woman. "I'd consider it an early Christmas present," she told Kristin.

The medical examiner pretended to roll her eyes. "If only the rest of the family was that easy to please."

"All you have to do is tell them your news and you can sit back and consider your holiday shopping done. Everyone will be thrilled."

Nodding, Kristin glanced over toward the other detective. He had become almost eerily quiet since she had turned over the preliminary copy of the autopsy report to him.

From the looks of it, he appeared to be absorbing every word that had been written down. "It's still rather sketchy," Kristin told Shayla's partner, apologizing for the lack of depth in the report.

After a beat, Gabriel realized that the medical examiner was addressing him and not his partner.

"That's okay," he assured her, looking up. "I can work with this. But call once you have the final copy."

Kristin nodded. "Will do."

Rather than remain behind as they walked out of the autopsy area, Kristin went out with them. Once outside the area, she deliberately drew her husband's cousin aside.

"How long have you been partnered up with this guy?" she asked, interested.

"Just since two days ago," Shayla answered. Gabriel had moved aside and was back to reading the report. "Why?"

"He's cute." Kristin kept her voice low, but there was definitely enthusiasm in it.

Shayla knew what was going on in the woman's head. Matchmaking seemed to be second nature to the Cavanaugh women once they had a ring on their own finger.

"Kristin, you're a married lady who's going to have her first baby," Shayla reminded her.

"All true, but I can still see—and appreciate. As I remember, your last partner was a patrolman who was on the verge of retirement—and looked a lot like Rip van Winkle," she added.

"And your point is?"

"Just that this guy is a huge improvement," she declared with approval. Leaning in, she whispered, "Don't let the grass start growing under your feet, that's all."

"You just take care of you and that little peanut growing inside, Kristin. I'll take care of me."

With that, Shayla moved over toward where her partner was leaning against the wall, still reading through the report. He had already gone through the report once and now appeared to be reviewing it for a second time.

"Let's go back to the squad room," she said to Cortland, using her regular speaking voice. "And go through that autopsy report." She saw that he was about to say something—most likely that he had already gone through the report—and she told him, "Some of us haven't had a chance to read it yet. We were too busy thanking the medical examiner for coming in and doing the autopsy for us."

Gabriel inclined his head, acknowledging her point.

"Sorry, I got caught up in the report," he confessed. Looking over his shoulder, he smiled at Kristin and said, "Thanks!"

"Don't mention it. As Shayla will tell you, that's what I'm here for," Kristin replied, returning to the autopsy room to collect her things.

Kristin was right, Shayla caught herself thinking as she looked at her partner just before they went back to the elevator. Cortland was really good looking.

Chapter 11

It was getting late, and Shayla felt that they weren't making all that much headway. Ordinarily, she would be inclined to call it a night, but she had a feeling that Cortland wasn't about to retreat. She had the impression that he would keep on working until he dropped.

Glancing to her right, she looked at him. He was still combing through his notes, as if he was hoping to find something that he had overlooked the first ten times.

Something occurred to her. "I take it that you've read the other autopsy reports on the Moonlight Killer's victims."

He hardly looked up. "I have," he answered dourly.

"Just how many victims were there?" she asked. She remembered reading a number, twelve, but somehow that didn't seem right.

"Too many," he replied, continuing to read his notes.

"I agree," Shayla said since in her opinion, even one murder qualified as too many.

"But in this case, what's the actual number?"

He put down the pages he was rereading. "Seventeen," he told his partner. "He killed one woman every few months—until his spree suddenly increased. And then he stopped." Gabriel tried to distance himself from the memory but found he still couldn't. "Looking back now, it seemed almost as if he was waiting to see if I was ever going to come back and play his sick game again."

She heard the pain in his voice. She wished she could back away from the topic altogether, but there were questions that needed to be answered if they were ever going to get this killer.

"You mean after he killed your wife and you went on that prolonged bender," Shayla guessed quietly.

For a moment, his eyes flashed, and then he said grimly, "Yeah."

"When you were in LA, were there other detectives working on the case as well?" she asked.

"Of course there were," he answered. "But once the Moonlight Killer's spree abruptly stopped and no more bodies turned up, there were other homicides that required more immediate attention. Some of the homicide squad even thought that maybe something had happened to him."

Shayla had stopped pretending to look at her notes. Her attention was completely riveted on her partner and what he was saying.

"But you didn't think that." It was more of a gut feeling than a guess.

He wasn't looking at her. Instead, he was staring into the air just above her head. He was in an entirely different place right now. "At the time, the only thing I could think of was that I had failed my wife, that she was dead because I wasn't there to protect her. I just wanted to drown that awful feeling of guilt any way I could. Suicide by bottle, I guess," he said cryptically with a shrug.

Shayla was utterly amazed that he was sharing this with her after having been so closemouthed and defensive up to this point. She had thought it would take her a lot longer and infinite patience to get him to open up. She hadn't counted on what an effect reading the autopsy report would have on him.

Shayla wanted to tell Cortland that she was touched to have him tell her all this, but that would be placing too much emphasis on the fact that he was verbalizing his pain. She decided it was better to make no comment on his revelation.

"Do you think the Moonlight Killer followed you out here?" she asked. "So that this sick game of his could continue?"

Cortland shrugged. He really didn't know for sure, but— "I guess it certainly looks that way," he told her. And then he shook his head disparagingly. "Not exactly the way I pictured my life going, being a serial killer's main adversary." He looked at Shayla. "But right now, there's no other way I *can* look at it. I need to end this man. Or at least his killing spree."

She had already assumed that Cortland had read all the other reports. "Did you get copies of the other autopsy reports and save them so you could look for possible overlapping similarities?" she asked. He struck her as someone who would do that. She knew she would in his place.

Gabriel laughed dryly in response. "One of the other detectives, a Guy Fergusson, accused me of having one hell of an odd hobby."

An odd hobby that could come in very handy, Shayla thought. Out loud she asked, "Did any of those reports make mention of that paralyzing drug that was administered to the convenience store clerk?" She couldn't help wondering if that was a new development or if the killer had used it all along and Cortland had only recently noticed it.

"Not to my knowledge," he admitted. "I only noticed that puncture mark behind the ear at the last scene in LA," he confessed, his face drawn and haunted-looking. "That's when I found that syringe on the floor. But at the time, I wasn't able to piece two sentences together, much less think clearly."

All he could think of at the time was that his wife was gone and his life was over.

Shayla had been exhausted a few moments ago thanks to all the work they had put in. Now her mind was racing.

"Is there any way the coroner who worked those cases could go back to run that test, looking for some sort of paralytic agent?"

He shook his head. "The only way the coroner could

do that was if he could get some of those bodies exhumed."

"Is that even possible?" she asked. Physically, she assumed that at least some of the victims had been buried rather than had their bodies cremated. But of the ones that had been buried, there would undoubtedly be all sorts of awful feelings attached to exhuming them, she couldn't help thinking.

"The next of kin for those victims would have to be approached and authorize the exhumation, but in the name of catching that bloodthirsty maniac, I'm sure some of them would agree." He could feel his own stomach tightening, but he knew that in his wife's case, he would have to agree to the exhumation. "It's not like they would have to witness it being done," he added.

"No," she agreed, "they wouldn't." The more she thought about it, the more it seemed like the way to go. Shayla nodded her head. "I think it might be a good idea to see if any of those people would be willing to have an exhumation done. We just need a few to say yes."

Gabriel had another idea. "Before we ask the department to go to the expense, both monetary and emotional, of digging up those bodies, why don't we go through the victims' autopsy reports to see if there was any mention made of defensive wounds found on those victims?"

"If there weren't any," Shayla concluded, "it might be a pretty good argument that the killer had rendered them immobile. Conversely, if the victims did have defensive wounds, that meant that the victim tried to fight him off. They wouldn't have been able to do that if they had been injected with that paralytic agent."

"Good point," he said. "I don't have those other autopsy reports here," he told her. "They're at my apartment."

That made sense, Shayla thought. "Well, it's well past quitting time," she pointed out. "Time for all good little detectives to call it a night and go home." She looked at her partner. "We could get started reading those reports first thing in the morning."

"We could," he agreed.

That did *not* sound convincing to her. "Why do I think you plan to be up all night, reading?" she asked.

He didn't bother confirming or denying her supposition. Instead, he said, "Because you're probably the most opinionated woman I've ever crossed paths with."

Rather than take offense, Shayla pretended he had meant it as a joke. "Flatterer."

Gabriel opened his mouth to say something, then closed it again, shaking his head. "It wasn't meant to be flattering."

Shayla's mouth curved. "I always try to make the best of a situation. Are you really determined to read through those reports you have tonight?"

He knew he could just dismiss her assumption, but he also knew that she wouldn't believe him. Those blue eyes of hers just seemed to have a way of looking straight into a man's soul.

The idea both intrigued him and made him uncomfortable.

Rather than answer her directly, he replied with a

question of his own to see how she would react. "And if I am?"

"You could invite me over so I could help you with all that reading. Autopsy reports make for unsettling reading, especially late at night."

What was she telling him? "You afraid of the dark?" he asked her.

"I was as a kid," she admitted.

"I never was," he told her, then explained his reasoning. "There's nothing there in the dark that wasn't there in the light."

She thought that over for a second, then asked, "Does that mean you were perpetually fearless, or that the idea of ghosts got under your skin just as much in the daylight as it did in the dark?"

How did the conversation turn into something so personal, he couldn't help wondering. He certainly hadn't tried to direct the subject toward a personal nature. As a matter of fact, he had done his best to keep things from veering into that territory.

But how could that have even been possible, he thought the next moment, given the fact that this whole thing was incredibly personal to him?

"Why don't we focus on what needs to be done and not on me?" he suggested.

"Okay," she agreed brightly. "Does that mean you're inviting me over? To help read those reports," she added when he made no effort to answer her question.

Gabriel looked as if he was actually considering her suggestion for a total of about five seconds before disregarding the entire idea. Although he had to admit—to himself and no one else—that she hadn't been as annoyingly overwhelming as he had expected her to be. Some of the things she had proposed had even made sense. Gabriel felt as if he should quit while he was ahead in this game, at least for now.

The autopsy that had been done today had taken more out of him than he had thought it would. While it did give credence to his theory, it also depressed him to no end, because it made him think about what Natalie had had to endure at the hands of this psycho, not to mention what their unborn baby had to have endured by proxy.

From the moment Natalie had told him she was pregnant, he had thought of the baby as a person in the making, with all the features, all the attributes of a child of his. He had been alone for most of his life, passed from one person to another while his mother searched for a way to enjoy her life and have someone take care of her.

The life he had been determined to forge with Natalie was going to be different, he had promised himself. All the pieces for that happiness had been put in place—and then this maniac had stolen it all from him. From Natalie.

It had been almost more than he could bear—until he had forced himself to focus on his renewed purpose—to avenge Natalie and all the victims who had died at this depraved man's hand.

"Why don't we get an early start tomorrow?" he suggested, thinking that he had put the topic to bed for now.

He saw her looking at him as if she could see answers there that he was trying to keep to himself.

"No offense, Cortland, but I still don't believe you," she told him. He was going to go through those reports, and she didn't want him doing that alone.

"What?" Cortland questioned, hoping she wasn't talking about what he thought she was talking about.

"You're not planning on getting an early start tomorrow. You are going to go home and start reading those reports the minute you close the door behind you," she told him. "I just figured two sets of eyes are better than one."

She gave him the impression of someone who was not about to back off. "I said I was going to get started tomorrow. Why won't you believe that?"

"Well, there is one way you could convince me," she told him.

Suspicion washed over him, but he was committed to playing this out. "Go ahead, I'm listening."

"Invite me over."

He scowled. "We've already gone through this," he informed her.

"Yes," she allowed. "But not to my satisfaction. And, if you're actually not planning on staying up to read those reports, I'll follow you home and you can just hand them to me. And I'll get started on them tonight."

He stared at her. The woman had to be kidding, he thought. "You want me to hand them over to you so you can take them over to your place?" he questioned, stunned that she could even suggest such a thing.

She could see the problem had multiple layers. She tried to strip it down to the basics.

"No, I can curl up on your couch and read the reports there. That way, they never actually leave your apartment, you can get some much-needed rest and the work can still get started. Did I manage to check all the right boxes?" she asked him cheerfully.

"All except for the one that you should be locked up in," he answered.

"We can talk about doing that later," she promised. "Right now, from what you mentioned earlier, there are a number of autopsy reports that need to be gone through, and I'm eagerly volunteering to do the reading."

His eyebrows drew together. "Eagerly?" he repeated incredulously.

"Well, maybe not eagerly, but my heart's definitely in the right place," she told him.

Gabriel snorted. "I'll take your word for it. Well, since I'd rather not have you breaking into my place in the middle of the night, you might as well come along."

"I really won you over?" she cried in surprise, pleased at having managed to turn him around to her way of seeing things.

They left the squad room and went down to the first floor, then proceeded to leave the building. He noticed that she had waved goodbye to the person manning the front desk. Was there no one this woman didn't know?

"No, it's more like you wore me out so I'll go along with this wild idea of yours—for now," he stipulated. He led the way down the stairs and to the parking area.

She deliberately ignored his last phrase. "Hey, I'm not greedy. A win is a win," she told him happily.

Gabriel sighed. "Whatever you say," he muttered dismissively.

"In the interest of that—" she began, only to have him cut her short.

"No," Gabriel declared, opening his vehicle door.

"But you don't know what I was going to say," she pointed out when he had so quickly shot her down. She got in the passenger side and buckled up.

"I don't care. Whatever it is, the answer's no," he told her.

She looked at him, innocence personified. "I was just going to suggest that we stop at a takeout place to pick up something to eat on the way to your place."

"Oh." He scowled at her for a moment as he drove away from the precinct. Leave it to her to have effectively taken the wind out of his sails, Gabriel thought. Refusing to agree didn't do either one of them any good. "I suppose we can do that," he said.

He saw the grin blooming on her face, and although he wanted to maintain his silence, he found that he couldn't. He needed to know what had prompted her to smile like that.

"What?"

"Nothing," Shayla said. She could feel herself smiling so hard, she was fairly sure that her cheeks were going to crack at any moment. "It's just that, considering how you feel about being partnered with someone, you seem to be coming along rather nicely," she told him.

Gabriel's hands tightened on the steering wheel.

Shayla's unwilling partner blew out a breath. For the time being, he felt it best just to keep his silence.

Chapter 12

Gabriel slowly raised his head as he opened his eyes.

He didn't remember falling asleep, but he obviously must have. Why else had his head wound up on the kitchen table, nestled between pages of the autopsy reports and the paper wrapper that initially had held a chicken salad sandwich?

His neck cracked a little, playing a symphony and reminding him that he wasn't ten years old anymore and that was why pillows had been invented—so that sane people wouldn't wake up feeling as if they had spent the night on a hard, unforgiving surface.

Gabriel rubbed his neck, trying to massage out the kink.

The first thought that hit him when his mind started to focus was that he wasn't alone. He remembered that

that annoying Cavanaugh woman had been here with him, reading reports as well.

Blinking, he scanned the room. He didn't see her at first, but he doubted that he could have been lucky enough for her to have gone back to her own lair.

Could he?

Just as a glimmer of hope began to rise in his chest, he saw her. She had made herself comfortable on his sofa, taking along her share of autopsy reports.

The glimmer of hope disappeared.

Although he tried to recall details, Gabe couldn't remember the woman curling up on the sofa.

Actually, he could barely remember anything after they had settled in and eaten the takeout food she had insisted that they pick up. He did remember announcing that he was going to read through the reports he had, and she had insisted that she take half of them.

But after that, the rest of the evening was all a blur. He must have been more tired than he'd thought, Gabriel decided.

Taking in another long breath, he got up and crossed over to stand next to the woman who seemed so bent on driving him crazy. Lying on the sofa like that, fast asleep and holding a report in her hand, she looked almost harmless.

Gabriel smiled to himself. He imagined that her coworkers probably thought the same thing about Typhoid Mary as she moved among them in the hospital kitchen where she had worked—spreading the disease.

Gabriel thought about waking his partner up, then

decided to enjoy the peace and quiet for a little while longer.

With that in mind, he moved soundlessly over to the coffee maker on the counter. Coffee would definitely help him wake up.

Gabriel measured out the necessary coffee grounds and was about to pour in a cup's worth of water when he stopped. Cavanaugh would probably want coffee, too. Muttering under his breath, he measured out more coffee before finally pouring in enough water to brew two cups rather than just one.

Within moments, the coffee maker began to make brewing noises.

"Smells good."

He turned around to see that his partner was sitting up on the sofa. So much for peace and quiet.

"It's nothing special," Gabriel told her.

She swung her legs off the sofa, and the papers she had been holding when she had fallen asleep went raining down onto the floor.

"Oh damn," she murmured, looking at the resulting chaos.

Gabriel crossed over to the pile of papers to pick them up at the exact same time that his partner bent over to do the same. The end result was that their heads collided rather unceremoniously.

Shayla could have sworn that she saw stars, and for a second, she lost her bearings and nearly her balance. Gabriel moved quickly and caught her by the shoulders in an attempt to steady her.

"Are you all right?" he asked, afraid that the collision might make her pass out.

Gabriel had surprised her by displaying the first concern she had heard from him. It managed to momentarily catch her up short.

"Oh yeah, I'm fine," she assured him, although she winced as she passed her hand over her forehead. Nevertheless, she denied any bad effects. "I've got a pretty hard head. Just ask any of my brothers—or my mom, for that matter," she added with a self-deprecating grin. "My mother runs an ambulance company, so she should know about things like that," she added, her eyes dancing in amusement.

Looking at her uncertainly, Cortland went to the freezer and took out an ice pack. The worn ice pack was a holdover from his drinking days. Holding on to it served as a reminder that he could never allow himself to go down that rabbit hole again—at least not until after he caught the Moonlight Killer and put the man away.

Filling it, Gabriel brought the ice pack back with him and held it out to his partner. "Here, apply that to your forehead before you have a bump on it the size of a small planet."

"I thought you were bringing the coffee," she said with a note of longing.

"This will do that bump on your forehead more good than the coffee," he said. Returning to the kitchen, he set out two cups and filled them. "I'm sorry about your head," he finally apologized.

"That's okay. It's not like you did it on purpose," she

told him. The next moment, applying the cold pack, she shivered. "This is really cold," she said. After several seconds had gone by, she held the ice pack away from her.

"Keep it on for at least five minutes," he instructed.

"I'm afraid it I do, it'll freeze my brain." Shayla was only half kidding.

"You never know, that might be a good thing," Gabriel commented, bringing the two cups of coffee over and placing them on the coffee table in front of the sofa.

"Is that humor?" she asked him in surprise. Shayla smiled. "I didn't know you had it in you."

Gabriel nodded toward the cup in front of her. "Drink your coffee," he said, sitting down on the far edge of the sofa.

When he saw Shayla getting up, he automatically put his hand on her wrist to stop her. The last thing he wanted was her falling down. "Where are you going?" he asked.

"I know you drink your coffee black, but I need milk in mine. I actually like cream better," she admitted, "but I figure that would be too much to hope for, so I was going to look for a container of milk."

She pulled a little, attempting to free her hand, but he continued holding it. A warm feeling began to inch its way up her arm, spreading out as it went.

"Sit," he ordered, rising to his feet to get her the milk. "What would be too much to hope for is for you to be quiet for at least a few minutes."

"More humor," Shayla commented, looking over toward her partner. "Granted, not enough for you to pack up and take your show on the road, but it is definitely a step in the right direction."

Gabriel shook his head at her droll assessment. "I guess you didn't get hit as hard as I thought," he said, setting a half pint of milk next to her coffee cup. "You're back to your usual babbling."

"Please," Shayla said, leaning forward a little so she could put some milk into her coffee, "you're making me blush." She pored over the pages that had caused them to collide in the first place. Gabriel had set them on the side of the coffee table. "I didn't find anything in my share of the autopsies, and by anything I mean mention of defensive wounds. Did you?"

"No," he answered flatly.

They both knew what that meant. Shayla put it into words first. "We've got a bunch of people to approach about exhuming their loved ones."

As an afterthought, she looked at the cup in her hands she had just sampled and said, "This is good."

"Just store-bought coffee," he told her, shrugging off her compliment. He had nothing to do with it other than opening the can.

"Must be the loving way it was prepared," she told him.

Heaven help him, he was practically getting used to her flippant remarks. Maybe that collision had affected him as well.

Draining his cup, he set it down and said, "Why don't I drop you off at the precinct so you can drive to your place, take a shower and then drive yourself over to the precinct?"

Shayla deliberately blinked her eyelashes at him. "Are you giving me the bum's rush, Detective?" she asked.

"No," he bit off. "What I'm being is practical."

"And what else are you going to be doing while I'm gone besides being practical?" she asked.

Shayla couldn't shake the feeling that he would use any excuse he could to ditch her and go off on his own in this investigation.

"I'm planning on taking my own shower before going back to the precinct," he told her. "Why, isn't that allowed? Or would you want to supervise my shower to make sure I do it right?"

For just the tiniest second, her mouth went dry. Where had that come from? And why was it creating these images in her head?

After a moment, she managed to form words. "I just wanted to make sure I went on working with you on this case. I have visions of you taking off," she admitted honestly.

His eyes met hers. He caught himself conjuring up a different sort of vision of his partner, just for a moment. The kind of vision that reminded him, if only for the smallest moment, that he was a man and not just a crime-fighting robot.

"I have no intentions of taking off," he informed her dryly. "Now, are you ready to go?"

"Just as soon as I rinse out my coffee cup," she told her partner, getting up with the empty cup.

"Leave the coffee cup," he ordered, sounding like a drill sergeant. "I know how to clean up."

And then he looked her over one final time as she rose to her feet. "Are you sure you're okay?"

His own head hurt a little and, in his opinion, she had sustained a much harder blow than he had. The last thing he needed or wanted was for the chief of detectives' niece to get hurt while in his care.

"I have a partner who knows how to clean up after himself as well as after me. I'm great," Shayla declared cheerfully.

Gabriel closed his eyes and shook his head, then looked at her. "You're crazy, you know that, right?"

Shayla grinned in response as she looked at him, then crossed toward the door and picked up her purse.

"Let's go, Gabriel. We're burning daylight."

"Daylight," he pointed out, nodding toward the front window, "just got here."

"Still, we're burning it nonetheless," she answered with authority. "You can't argue with that."

"Apparently," he told her wearily, "you can—and do—argue with absolutely anything, and everything."

"Not true," she told him as she followed him out the door.

"See, you're even arguing about this," Gabriel pointed out.

Shayla decided that, for the time being, the best way for her to proceed was just not to say anything.

Because he was concend about the bump on the head she had received, once she picked up her car at the precinct, he decided to follow her to her house—just in case.

Gabriel pulled up in front of Shayla's house. The recently painted building was located in one of the older residential developments in Aurora, one of the first five that had been built at the time the city had been incorporated.

He noted that her house was a single-story model, and, in a state where land was quickly going at a premium, he was surprised to see just how large a plot her house was sitting on.

Gabriel had planned to just stop his vehicle and look around, then quickly take off back to his own place, but his curiosity aroused, he just had to ask her.

"Does this land all belong to the house?" He knew that in some residential areas, they had something referred to as a zero property line, where the land on one side of the house or the other actually belonged to the house that was located right next door. Supposedly it was to make the yards the houses were on just appear bigger, although he thought of the whole thing as being some sort of a visual trick.

Gabriel's question caught her off guard for a moment, but then she realized what he was asking her.

"It doesn't belong to the house," she corrected him. "The lot the house is standing on belongs to me."

Gabriel had just assumed his partner was renting the house, especially since she was so young. "You own this house?" he asked her incredulously.

"Well, the bank and I do," Shayla told him. "But eventually, it'll be all mine when I pay it off."

In his estimation, she seemed too young to be a homeowner. The only people he knew who weren't renters were older family men with kids—kids they were attempting to convince to go to college. These Cavanaughs, Gabriel decided, were a whole different breed than what he was normally accustomed to.

As if reading her partner's mind, Shayla told him, "My mother thought it was a good idea for all her kids to buy a house as soon as they were financially able to make a down payment. When my father was killed in the line of duty and she had to go back to work, my mother decided that each of us needed to have something stable to hang on to—other than each other and the rest of the family, of course," she added with a smile. "My mother is a really great believer in earning your own way. She always has been."

Gabriel nodded, barely listening. His mind was already back on the case. He needed to make a list of people to get in contact with, as well as putting together the professions that would allow someone to get their hands on the drug that was used without attracting attention.

"I'm going to get going," he announced, his body language saying that for all intents and purposes, he was already gone.

"I'll hurry," Shayla promised needlessly. "I'll see you back in the squad room."

Gabriel barely nodded. "Yeah."

Starting up his car, he was just about to drive off when his cell phone suddenly began ringing. He turned off the engine and took out his phone.

Just as hers started to ring as well.

She looked at Gabriel through his window. They were being summoned into the precinct, she thought.

Any other explanation just seemed like too much of a coincidence.

"I think our showers just got put on hold," Shayla said, taking out her phone.

Gabriel was already talking on his.

"Cavanaugh," she declared, swiping her phone on.

"There's been another killing," the deep voice on the other end of her phone said. "The victim was tied up just like the convenience store clerk."

Chapter 13

Shayla put her cell phone away in her small shoulder bag. Cortland had already slipped his into his pocket. There was silence for a moment as their eyes met.

"This isn't normal, is it?" she asked through his opened window, fairly sure that she knew the answer before her partner said anything.

"The guy's a homicidal maniac," Gabriel answered. The disgust was meant for the serial killer, not for the woman who had just gotten out of his car. "There's not a damn thing normal about him."

Shayla shook her head. "I meant timing wise. He doesn't usually kill his victims so close together, does he?" Something was up, and she hated thinking about what that might mean.

"No," Gabriel answered her grimly. "He doesn't."

She looked over toward her vehicle, parked in her driveway. "Should we just drive back to the precinct in yours?" she asked.

Leaning all the way over to his right, Gabriel strained to reach toward the passenger side and threw open the passenger door for her.

"Get in," he instructed.

"Well, since you asked so nicely," she began, trying to inject a little humor into what was a completely humorless moment. She stopped short when she saw the impatient look creasing his brow. "I'm getting in, I'm getting in," Shayla told him, sliding into the passenger seat and pulling the door closed behind her.

Shayla was still securing her seat belt when her partner took off. Instead of sitting in her seat, she found herself sliding first to the right and then the left as Gabriel tore out of the development. Even when she finally did secure her seat belt, the ride she was on couldn't exactly be described as a very stable one.

To finally stop moving so erratically, Shayla firmly braced her hands against the dashboard. She was just grateful that she hadn't had breakfast yet, although the coffee she'd had at his apartment wasn't exactly sitting all too well in her stomach. She understood why he might be in a hurry, but he really needed to slow down a little.

"Do you charge extra for this?" she asked, doing her best to hold on as Gabriel made another fast turn.

"No," Gabriel bit off, making it clear that this was no time for any of her so-called witty humor.

Her eyes widened as he took another really fast turn.

"I think you took the wrong turn," she told him, read-ing the street signs as they whizzed by. "This isn't the way to the precinct."

"I know," he answered. "It's the way to the crime scene." With that, Cortland made a rather unnerving turn at the end of the block.

"You know where the crime scene is?" she asked, surprised. No mention of that had been made in the call she had gotten.

"Garza told me," Gabriel said, referring to one of the detectives he had been introduced to in the last couple of days. All their faces had merged together, but their voices had set them apart. "He was the one who took the initial call."

"So?" Was he going to keep her guessing? "Where is the crime scene?"

"The victim's body was found in the stacks in the university library," he told her, then gave her the details that Garza had passed on to him. "One of the librarians found her when she came in early to open up," he said. Gabriel spared her a glance just before he took another left turn, this time making his way directly onto the university campus. "Now you know as much as I do."

When Shayla made no response, he looked at her again, reminding himself that she had received a rather substantial bump on her head when their heads had un-ceremoniously collided. Maybe it was interfering with her ability to process information. "Are you up to this, or should I have dropped you off at the precinct first?"

She saw that he was more than ready to turn back. "I'm fine," she quickly assured him. "And I'm a great deal better off than that poor woman the librarian found in the stacks." This whole thing had her wondering again about the killer they were dealing with. "Why do you think the Moonlight Killer has upped his game?"

Her partner frowned. He wished she'd stop asking questions. "My guess is that he's trying to make up for lost time," he told her.

"You mean for those nine months you dropped out?" she asked bluntly. She knew the question made him uncomfortable, but these were questions that needed to be answered so they knew if they were ultimately going in the right direction. "Why do you think he singled you out this way?" There had to be a reason why the killer was so fixated on Cortland.

Gabriel shrugged. "Who knows? Maybe I got closer to finding him than the other detectives did." Reaching his destination, he pulled up in a parking spot near the library.

Getting out of the car, Gabriel took out his badge and detective ID, preparing to show them to the police officer who was approaching them. It was obvious that the latter was about to tell them that they had to move their vehicle and couldn't enter the crime scene.

Looking at Cortland's badge and identification, the officer gave Shayla a confused look. She quickly followed suit.

Satisfied, the uniformed officer waved them on their way, saying, "Everyone and his brother wants to see what's going on," by way of an explanation for why he'd been about to bar them a moment ago.

"At least they're still alive to do that," Gabriel commented.

The officer nodded. "Yeah, I guess that's one way to look at it." He followed the two Aurora detectives as they headed toward the library entrance. "You want me to get one of the officers to show you to the stacks?" he asked, explaining, "I've got to stay out here."

"That won't be necessary," Shayla answered. "I know where the stacks are. I graduated from this university."

Gabriel turned to look at her. "You went to school here?"

She didn't know if he was impressed or about to say something disparaging. Most likely the later, she decided. "I did."

Gabriel stepped to the side and gestured for her to go through the entrance first. "Then, by all means, lead the way, Cavanaugh," he told her.

She took the steps leading to the front doors quickly. She couldn't remember how many times she had been here, studying or writing papers. Never once had she ever thought this would be the site of a murder.

"I always figured I'd come back here someday, but not because I had to investigate a crime scene," she confessed sadly. Shayla looked around as she was about to enter, memories flooding her mind. "This always seemed like a safe space to me."

"Just shows that you can never take anything for granted," Gabriel told her.

There was another police officer posted at the library's entrance. Seeing their badges, she quickly stepped aside.

"You'll find the victim all the way downstairs," the police officer told them, then warned, "Brace yourselves."

Gabriel stopped and looked at the young woman. "Why?"

The police officer shrugged, somewhat embarrassed by her reaction. But she answered the solemn-looking detective.

"It's the stuff nightmares are made of," she told him. "At least mine will be from here on in," she lamented. The woman's voice dropped as she confided to Shayla, "I think I picked the wrong line of work."

"Well, I hate to tell you, but it doesn't get any easier," Shayla told her. "But after a while, you develop a tougher skin and find that you can put up with things a lot better."

Pointing toward where they needed to go, the officer remained at her post. "The poor librarian found the victim tied up and at the bottom of the stacks. She screamed so loudly, several people called 911."

"Is the librarian still downstairs?" Shayla asked. "We'll need to ask her some questions after we view the victim." Shayla couldn't get herself to say, "dead body." Somehow, calling the poor young woman that just felt too disrespectful. The victim had been a human being, most likely a student, with a life. A life that had been cut far too short, Shayla thought.

"I think her name is Josephine," the officer interjected. "After Josephine finally stopped screaming, she was shaking so badly, one of the other officers called for an ambulance and had her taken to the ER. She's probably still there now."

Shayla could see that Gabriel was anxious to go downstairs into the stacks to see the victim for himself. Thanking the officer for the information, Shayla told her, "We'll go there when we're done here."

The young woman nodded. "The crime scene investigators are already down in the stacks," the officer said, adding, "They just got here a few minutes before you two did."

Shayla didn't remember seeing the CSI vehicle, but she knew that there was parking available on three sides of the library, so she could have easily missed it. She had been focused on getting here as quickly as she could and viewing the crime scene while it was still relatively fresh.

"Thank you," she said to the officer. "You've been a great help."

The young woman beamed at the compliment. It was obvious to the Shayla that the officer's ego could use a little bolstering.

Gabriel looked as if he was straining at the bit and walked into the building ahead of her.

The area was wide-open and airy, perhaps just slightly smaller than she recalled. Shayla could remember getting lost here a number of times in her first year at the university. Now it all seemed so familiar—and it had been violated by the Moonlight Killer, she thought angrily. He had taken what had once been such a safe space to her and turned it into a place of unimaginable horror.

She had to struggle to keep herself from being overwhelmed with waves of anger. Striding toward the stairs leading into the stacks, Shayla glanced over her shoulder to make sure she hadn't lost Gabriel.

He was still looking around, methodically taking everything in. She could tell by his expression that Gabriel was viewing it all through the victim's eyes. Shayla could only guess what was going through her partner's mind, but she felt for him.

"This way," she told her partner, leading the way to a stairwell off to the side.

Gabriel's pace quickened until he had caught up with her. Shayla was moving down the stairs quickly, her heels clicking almost rhythmically against the metal.

Gabriel was right behind her.

There wasn't really enough room for two people to go down together. The stairway, he noted, had a rather dated appearance, like it had been initially put in when the university had been built, some forty-odd years ago.

Despite the fluorescent lights illuminating the stairs and beyond, there was a somber darkness to the area that only grew more so the farther down they went.

By the time they reached the bottom of the second stairway, she could make out the sound of voices, talking.

"I guess we're the last to get here," Shayla commented to her partner. Gabriel merely grunted in response.

Shayla saw that her uncle had come out to review the scene with his team again. Usually, he varied his involvement, sending someone else to head the team if he had come out the day before. But here he was, leading his team again. Apparently, her uncle had made catching the serial killer a personal priority, just the way Gabriel and she had.

Sean Cavanaugh raised his eyes when he saw the two detectives approaching him. "We've got to stop meeting this way," he commented sadly.

"Tell me about it," Shayla said.

Rather than answer her, Sean looked toward his niece's partner. "You're the expert here, Cortland. Is this the Moonlight Killer's usual mode of operation, to practically follow up one killing with another, or is this something new for him?"

Gabriel had walked by the CSI team, who were cataloging the various data that had been found at the crime scene, even though that data proved to be scarce.

Gabriel seemed intent on absorbing everything. Finally, he turned toward Sean.

"This is something new," he admitted. He had really hoped that the Moonlight Killer would have reduced his pace and that he would be caught before he killed again.

No such luck, Gabriel decided.

"Well, maybe since the Moonlight Killer has stepped up his game, he'll get sloppy and that'll give us more of a fighting chance," Sean theorized.

Gabriel allowed himself to savor that thought, although he had some grave doubts.

"Maybe," Shayla's partner said without any real conviction.

So far, Shayla thought, turning back to the victim, who had been roped and tied up in the same unnerving fashion as her predecessors, there seemed to be no connection between the young women, other than the fact that they were all in a certain age range.

Beyond that, there was no similarity in looks, nationality or what they did for a living. And, from what she had managed to learn, the women had nothing in common. The victims had been employed in a wide range of work.

Gabriel's wife, she recalled reading, had taken a leave of absence three months into her pregnancy because she had felt too tired to be able to do a good job. She had been fighting a constant battle against fatigue.

Maybe if the woman had remained working, she wouldn't have been in the wrong place at the wrong time and caught the killer's eye.

Gabriel bent down, getting as close to the victim as he could. As he shone the small, powerful flashlight he always had in his possession along her body, he didn't detect any defensive wounds on her hands.

"What are you looking for?" Sean asked as he turned around to see Gabriel conducting what appeared to be a methodical search of the victim's body.

Shayla began to answer for her partner, then pressed her lips together. This was Cortland's show. It was up to him to answer her uncle.

"Whether or not the woman has any defensive wounds on her," Gabriel answered, "and if there's any evidence of a drug being administered."

As Shayla and her uncle watched, her partner slowly went over every square inch of the victim's upper body—until he finally found what he was looking for.

Chapter 14

"There it is," Gabriel declared, moving to the extreme right so that the head of the crime scene investigative team could see what he had managed to locate.

Gabriel pointed to the area where the needle had gone in to inject the paralyzing agent into the victim.

The injection had created a minuscule pinprick at the very back of her neck. The injection had turned that small area into a rather angry shade of pink.

Obviously, Gabriel concluded, the victim had been allergic to the paralytic agent that had been used on her.

"I thought that was an insect bite. I was going to ask the coroner if I was right or if that was caused by something other than a bug," Sean said to the two detectives. He looked at his niece's partner. "Nice catch."

Gabriel shrugged off the compliment. To him a "nice

catch" would have been applicable if he had managed to capture the serial killer.

"It helps if you know what you're looking for," he told the head of the investigative team.

Gabriel looked around on the floor, but found no syringe.

"What are you looking for?" Sean asked, pausing to look on the library floor as well.

"The last couple of times, the Moonlight Killer discarded the syringe with the paralyzing agent he used. This time it looks like he took the syringe with him— or threw it out someplace," Gabriel theorized.

Shayla had trouble looking away from the victim. The woman looked so young. She'd obviously had her whole life before her—until it had been brutally stolen from her.

She turned toward her uncle. "Do we have a name for the victim yet?" Shayla asked.

"Amanda Quinn. She was working on her master's thesis in English literature. It was on the evolution of comedy," Destiny Cavanaugh, Sean's right-hand assistant as well as his daughter-in-law, volunteered the information. "I looked through her backpack, trying to find her name."

Gabriel gazed down at the victim's face. "There are no defensive wounds," he noted. Just like the last victim. This woman had apparently been dead a number of hours. "She never even saw this coming. Most likely, the killer has to wear soft-soled sneakers." Rising, he turned toward Shayla. "We need to talk to that librarian who found the victim—and to anyone who might have been on duty late last night."

His eyes swept over the scene, taking it all in. This time, the Moonlight Killer had tied up the victim and hung her from one of the massive library shelves. "Maybe we'll get lucky and find someone who saw something." Although he had to admit, he had his doubts. He turned to look at his partner again. "Students don't have to sign in to use the library anymore, do they?"

Shayla had heard that was once a thing, but not for a very long time. "Not for years and years," she told him, then she looked at her cousin's wife. "Are there any surveillance cameras around?"

Destiny looked as disappointed as Shayla felt. She shook her head. "I already asked. The students said they felt as if the people in charge were spying on them, so the cameras were all taken down or disconnected."

Shayla's eyes met her partner's. It was hard to say which of them was more disappointed. "Too bad. A little bit of spying might have come in handy right about now," she said. "It could have helped us get this guy instead of having him out there, hunting for more victims."

Sean Cavanaugh was taking photographs of the victim from several different angles. Gabriel waited until the man paused. "We're going to need to see the autopsy report as soon as it's available," he told the CSI head, stressing, "I need the coroner to have the lab test Amanda's blood for any and all neuromuscular blocking agents."

Sean looked very interested. "Is that what you think was used on the victim?"

"Victims," Gabriel corrected, stressing the plural. "To my knowledge, at least two of the last two victims before this one were injected with a paralytic agent, instantly rendering them unable to fight back. In all likelihood, there were more victims that were injected," he added. "If that turns out to be the case, the information could help us narrow down the list of people to look into and investigate. A neuromuscular blocking agent isn't something just anyone can get their hands on."

Sean turned toward his niece, smiling. "Looks like you got partnered up with a good one right out of the gate," he told her, nodding his head with approval.

"What was your uncle talking about?" Gabriel asked as, armed with the name of the hospital the librarian had been taken to, he and Shayla made their way out of the library stacks.

She realized that Cortland had probably forgotten this fact. She was fairly certain that she had told him this on their first day. "He was referring to the fact that you are my first partner since I passed my exam and got my detective's shield," she explained. She saw doubt enter his eyes and quickly said, "Don't let the fact that I'm a newbie bother you. I grew up surrounded by detectives and absorbed an awful lot facts and procedures just through osmosis."

The grin she flashed at him was all but disarming. It took him a moment to tear his eyes away.

"Yeah, right," he muttered dismissively.

"No, really," Shayla insisted. "Every family gathering we ever had—and there have been an awful lot of them—the older generation always talked shop. That went on until we suddenly *became* the older generation."

He shrugged, trying to appear as if he was indifferent, even though he really wasn't—and that did bother him. "Whatever. I guess I'm stuck with you for the time being."

She wondered if that meant that he was going to attempt to get another partner. She really doubted that he would—at least, not until they could bring down the Moonlight Killer. Cortland had too much of himself invested in this, and she was fairly certain that he knew she could be an asset, not a liability, in this pursuit.

Once upstairs in the main library area, Shayla and Cortland went in search of the person in charge, a Mary Ann Elder, according to one of the officers. Miss Elder looked as if she could very well remember the days when students had to sign in before availing themselves of any of the books in the stacks. After showing the woman their shields and IDs, Shayla told the head librarian, "We need to find out who was working here on the late shift last night and if any of those people saw anything out of the ordinary at that time," Shayla asked.

The woman looked as if she would rather talk to Gabriel instead of his partner, but she forced herself to address Shayla's question. "Josephine Juarez had the late shift last night," she told the detectives.

"Josephine," Gabriel repeated. "Isn't she the young

woman who had the first shift here this morning?" he questioned.

"Yes," Mary Ann answered. "She was pulling a double shift. Josephine is getting married next year and asked me for extra work so she could save up as much money as she could." The woman dropped her voice, as if she was about to impart some great secret. "If you ask me, the gown she's buying is far too expensive, but then, nobody asked me." The woman sighed, as if this had all happened just to annoy her. "Now I have no idea if she's up to working at all, and I'll need to find someone who can come in and sub for her."

"In other words, this Josephine person is the only one we can talk to about what went on here last night?" Gabriel asked.

Mary Ann beamed at him. "You catch on quickly, Detective."

Shayla took out her card and placed it on the desk in front of the librarian. "If you or any of the other people who work here remember anything at all, please give me a call and let me know." Turning away, she looked at Gabriel. "Let's see if we can go talk to Josephine at the hospital," she proposed.

She felt that spending the extra minutes here had turned out to be a waste of time. Hopefully, the young woman in the ER could tell them something more helpful.

As they began to walk out of the library, Shayla looked at her partner. "Do you know how to get to the hospital from here?"

He hated to admit it, but he had no choice since he was the one who was driving. "No, not offhand."

"It's not that far from here," she told him. "I'll give you directions."

He laughed shortly. "I figured you would," he answered, hurrying down the stairs, away from the library.

Gabriel lost no time in getting to the parking lot. When he didn't hesitate but went directly to where he had parked his vehicle, Shayla had to admit that she was impressed. With three sides to the library parking lot, she had gotten lost finding her car the first few times when she had used the library.

Gabriel, on the other hand, seemed to have unerring instincts when it came to finding the vehicle. Opening the doors, he got into his car and waited for her to do the same.

As she settled in, he told her, "Okay, start giving me those directions."

She pretended to pout. "You're taking all the fun out of it. Isn't your manhood supposed to make you grumble about having to ask for directions?"

"My manhood is very secure," Gabriel informed her.

"Good to hear," she told him with a wide smile. Glancing at her, he got the impression that she actually meant it.

Shayla watched as her partner put his key in the ignition. "You know, we could just trade places and I could drive us there."

"My manhood might be secure," he told her, "but I haven't taken leave of my senses. I'll drive. Now, left or right?"

"Neither," she told him. "Just go straight until I tell you where to turn."

He slanted a look in Shayla's direction. "You're enjoying this, aren't you?"

Her eyes were twinkling. "Maybe just a little."

She had to give her partner a few more directions, which incorporated several more turns, before they were finally able to pull up in the hospital parking lot.

"You know, the streets here are a lot less busy than they are in Los Angeles," he couldn't help commenting. "In LA it feels like I'm practically driving around in circles. The streets in Aurora seem like they're a lot more straightforward," he said in quiet appreciation.

In the parking lot, Gabriel found a parking space some distance away from the actual ER entrance.

The moment he parked his car, he and Shayla immediately got out and hurried directly toward the emergency room entrance. The dark gray electronic doors sprang open the moment they came close to them.

There was a middle-aged woman sitting behind the admissions desk. She seemed rather harried, and it wasn't even nine in the morning yet. Shayla wondered if it had been very busy in the ER or if this was just the way the clerk normally looked—like a wilting flower.

To save time, both Shayla and Gabriel had their IDs and shields out as they approached the woman behind the desk.

"Did a Josephine Juarez come into the ER this morning? She would have been brought in by ambulance from the UC Aurora library," Shayla explained, adding, "According to the police officers on the scene, she had been rather badly traumatized."

The description immediately struck a nerve. "Oh yes, she came in and she's still here." The woman looked at her monitor to confirm something before she disclosed the information. "It took Dr. Benjamin a long time to finally calm her down. She just wouldn't stop wailing and crying."

"Where is she?" Shayla asked, immediately following that up with another question. "Can we see her?"

The receptionist turned from her desk and called over to one of the nurses who was leaving with a tablet. The latter kept glancing at the screen, reading something on it even as she was walking away.

"Donna," the reception called to her, "can you take these two officers—"

"Detectives," Shayla corrected the receptionist before her partner could speak up. She was afraid that he might see the "demotion" as an insult for some reason.

"—these two detectives," the receptionist corrected, "to see that woman who was brought in from the UC Aurora library? Josephine Juarez," the receptionist clarified. "I think they put her in bed number twelve in the ER."

The heavyset older woman nodded her head, her short-cropped dark hair bobbing around her face. Tucking the tablet under her arm, Donna told the pair that had been entrusted to her, "If you just come this way," and then turned on her rubber-soled heel.

"Do you know if Josephine said anything to anyone about what happened?" Shayla asked the older woman.

Donna shook her head. "Far as I know, the poor thing was too busy screaming to say anything actually coherent," Donna replied. "We don't even know what happened to her." She glanced over her shoulder at the two detectives. "The doctor couldn't get her to stop screaming and crying long enough to tell anyone why she was having this breakdown. Would you know?"

Shayla glanced at her partner. She felt that it was really more his story to tell than hers if he wanted to.

"Josephine Juarez came across the Moonlight Killer's latest victim. The victim was down in the library stacks at the time," Gabriel finally said when he realized that Shayla was waiting for him to take the lead. "It's a pretty unsettling sight," he said, deliberately leaving out the more unnerving details. "I can see why the poor woman would freak out the way she did."

"In your medical opinion, do you think that she will be able to talk to us?" Shayla asked the nurse.

She didn't want to make things worse for the traumatized young woman, but she was anxious to talk to possibly the only witness that they had—if the woman had actually even seen anything.

"It certainly is worth a try," Donna said, bringing them over to a curtained cubicle. All the beds in this part of the ER were equally divided. There were more empty beds than Shayla had thought there would be.

"Slow day?" Shayla asked, looking toward the nurse.

"It's the middle of the week. It'll pick up in a few hours," Donna predicted.

The nurse brought the two detectives over to the young woman who had had the misfortune of discovering the body hanging from the bookcase. "These detectives are here to see you, Josephine," Donna told the woman in the hospital bed, smiling at her.

Josephine Juarez slowly turned her head in their direction.

The disoriented look on her face quickly turned to one of abject terror.

Chapter 15

Josephine Juarez appeared as if she desperately wanted to disappear into the bedding. Her breathing became much more labored, and her eyes darted back and forth between the two strangers at her bedside.

"Go away. I didn't see anything. Please go away," she begged frantically. It seemed as if she was saying those words to Cortland.

Watching the librarian's reaction, Shayla made a quick judgment call. "Cortland, could you step away for a few minutes and meet me out in the hallway? I'd like to have a word alone with Ms. Juarez."

To be honest, she half expected her new partner to fight her on this. But to her surprise, Gabriel nodded his head, walked away and disappeared down the hall without a word.

The moment Cortland left, Shayla immediately turned her attention back to the distraught librarian. The woman had acted far too agitated around her partner. Something just didn't add up here.

"Josephine," she said in a soft, kind voice, "are you sure you didn't see anyone in the stacks before you went down there this morning?"

"No, not this morning," she denied, shaking her head.

"But...?" Shayla let her voice trail off as she waited for the librarian to offer more information.

Josephine swallowed hard, forcing herself to speak. "But he...bumped into me...as I was leaving the library last night." Her voice was trembling again, as if she felt she had said something she was going to wind up paying for.

"He?" Shayla cocked her head and looked at the young woman quizzically.

The librarian's voice dropped down to barely a whisper, not wanting to be overheard as she said, "Your partner."

"Detective Cortland?" Shayla questioned. "*He* was the man who bumped into you?"

She nervously pressed her lips together and finally answered, "Yes. Last night. It was around nine o'clock. I was in a hurry to leave, and I walked right into him. He looked surprised to see there was someone there—surprised to see me," she explained, "but he didn't say anything."

Shayla didn't protest or say that it couldn't have happened that way because at that time Cortland was with her in his apartment. That was when they were reviewing the pile of autopsy reports.

Instead, she calmly asked Josephine, "You're sure it was him?"

"Yes," the woman answered, although she did shrug her shoulders somewhat helplessly. But then she went on to describe the man she had bumped into. "Tall, muscular, dark hair." And then she shrugged again as if to explain why her description wasn't more detailed. "It happened really fast."

"Go on," Shayla urged gently, trying not to sound too eager as she continued to entertain the idea that had presented itself to her. "Tell me everything."

The devastated young librarian looked somewhat at a loss. "That's all there is to tell." Josephine pressed her lips together to keep from crying again. "Until I came in this morning and saw...and saw..." The young woman couldn't bring herself to finish her sentence.

Shayla patted the distressed librarian's hand, trying to comfort the other woman as best she could.

"Ms. Juarez, would you mind if I sent in a sketch artist to see you so you could give her a description of the person you saw in the library last night?" Shayla paused, then added, "It would be a really great help to us."

The librarian seemed confused by the request, but she nodded even as she said, "He looked like the detective who was in here with you."

"Still, it would help to have a sketch," Shayla said. And then she looked back at the nurse. "Is Ms. Juarez going to stay here for the day?"

Donna responded, "The doctor wants to run the patient through a battery of tests to check her out. If everything turns out to be negative, then the hospital will be able to release her and send her home. Most likely by tomorrow morning."

Taking all this in, Shayla nodded, then looked back at the woman in the hospital bed. "We'll send in that sketch artist to see you later on today, Ms. Juarez," she promised. Giving Josephine's hand another squeeze, she told the young woman who had, mercifully, stopped trembling, "I'll see you later today."

With that, Shayla walked out of the ER treatment area. Making her way down the hallway, she looked around to see if she could spot her partner somewhere.

He was nowhere to be found.

This was what she got for not being specific, Shayla upbraided herself. She should have told Cortland that she would meet him at the vending machine or some other more precise location.

"So," a deep voice from behind her said out of the blue, "what did the librarian wind up telling you?"

Startled, Shayla swung around, her flying blond hair all but whipping her partner in the face. She managed to comb it back with her fingers.

"You really need to make more noise when you're sneaking up on a person," she told him.

"Then it wouldn't be sneaking up, would it?" he challenged. There was just the barest touch of amusement in his voice.

Shayla spread her hand out on her chest. "Just let my heartbeat go back down to normal."

Taking a deep breath, she waited for a second until her heartbeat *did* settle down. She took another deep breath before she felt ready to answer his question.

This, she knew, wasn't going to be easy.

"I've got some good news and some bad news," she told her partner. "Oddly enough," she went on as she saw his eyebrows draw together quizzically, "it's the same news."

Gabriel frowned slightly. "You certainly know how to keep someone on pins and needles," he commented dryly. "Since it's the same news, out with it."

"I think we might have a clue as to what this guy looks like," Shayla began, choosing her words carefully. She also felt as if his eyes were drilling right into her.

"Go on," he told her.

Shayla pressed her lips together as she raised her eyes to his face.

"According to the librarian, the reason for her freaked-out reaction when we walked into the room together is that Josephine Juarez swears she bumped into the Moonlight Killer at the library last night."

Her partner paused. It was like waiting for a shoe to drop in slow motion.

"And?" he asked, never taking his eyes from her face.

"*And* she said that the man she bumped into was you," Shayla said, continuing to look at him for his reaction to this piece of news.

"Was *me*?" he questioned in complete and total disbelief.

"That's what she said."

"That's not possible," Gabriel denied. "I wasn't any-

where near that library last night—or ever before this
morning, for that matter."

"I *know* that. I'm your alibi, remember?" Shayla
pointed out—which was a good thing, she thought.
Because if they hadn't been together last night all the
way up to and including to when they had received the
call to come in today, she might have been tempted to
entertain some doubts about her partner's innocence.

But any possible doubts had been entirely wiped out
before they could even form, because she and Cortland
had spent all that time together.

That fact brought her to only one possible conclusion. She shared her suspicions with her partner before
this whole thing could get more out of hand.

"Everyone out there supposedly has a doppelgänger,"
she told him. "That's when—"

"I know what a doppelgänger is, Cavanaugh. Are you
saying that our witness actually thinks that she saw me
at the library last night?"

"I'm saying that Josephine admitted to being in a
hurry and that as she was dashing out, she bumped
into a tall, handsome, broad-shouldered man she could
have very easily mistaken for you in her haste to leave
the library."

Listening to this, his expression grew very solemn.
"That explains things," he said more to himself than
to his partner.

It had always bothered him that it appeared Natalie had let her killer into the house. If the Moonlight
Killer resembled him, that would have given him just

enough advantage and time to get the drop on Natalie and kill her.

The thought made him incredibly sick to his stomach.

Shayla was looking at Cortland's face. She could tell by his expression that he had gone to a very dark place and, if he was going to be of any use to himself and to her, she needed to get him out of there.

"Wherever you are, come back," Shayla ordered him. "We've finally been given a lead to work, and we need to use it to our benefit."

Gabriel assessed his partner. She was right. He couldn't allow himself to sink back into that quicksand bog that had threatened to swallow him up whole.

Taking a breath, as if that would help him clear his mind, Gabriel looked at her and asked, "Handsome, huh?"

She had been trying to figure out what was going on in his mind. His question managed to throw her.

"What?"

"You just used the word *handsome* to describe me," Gabriel pointed out.

"Josephine used the word, I didn't," she told him. "Just think of the word as a placeholder. I told our witness that I would send in a sketch artist to draw the man she passed in the library. Once she does, we can get started showing that sketch around to the library staff." Her eyes widened as she thought of something else. "And to any of the people who might have used the convenience store where our last victim was found.

"Who knows, maybe our killer stakes out his victims? He strikes me as being too methodical to just walk in cold and kill his victims without planning ahead. He doesn't seem like the type to do that," she told her partner.

Gabriel was inclined to agree with her. If the Moonlight Killer hadn't been so careful and had just been consumed with this overwhelming desire to kill, Gabriel was certain that the man would have been caught a lot sooner.

Maybe even before he had killed Natalie.

Gabriel dismissed the paralyzing thought. He wouldn't be able to get anywhere if that event remained front and center in his mind.

When they got back to the precinct, their first order of business was to report to their lieutenant.

Hollandale looked pleased to see them and impressed at the headway they seemed to have made. And it also surprised the lieutenant to hear that the witness currently in the ER had almost gone into shock when she saw Cortland come walking into the room.

When he finished listening to everything Shayla had to say, Hollandale remarked, "Lucky thing you had Cavanaugh to vouch for your whereabouts, Cortland." The librarian's accusation could have raised quite a few questions and gotten pretty messy before it was cleared up, the lieutenant thought. "Bet you're glad now that I didn't listen to you when you said you didn't want to be partnered up with Cavanaugh."

Gabriel had no choice but to agree. He nodded. "I

guess it would have made things really complicated otherwise."

Shayla grinned as they walked away from the lieutenant's office. "I didn't know you had a gift for understatement."

Gabriel decided it was safest just to ignore her.

"Want to grab some lunch?" Shayla asked after a moment.

He blew out a long breath, searching for patience. The emotion continued being among the missing. "What I want to do," he finally said, "is get to work."

Now that they had something to work with, Gabriel found he was more anxious than ever to continue following up leads on the murders. Eventually, they would have to take him somewhere.

"Okay," Shayla responded cheerfully, "we'll compromise and pick up some takeout."

That hadn't been a choice he was entertaining, but he knew she was probably right. Even a train needed fuel to keep going, he conceded.

"You pick the place," he told her.

Her grin grew wider. "Isn't it nice when we cooperate?" she told her partner with enthusiasm.

He slanted a look in her direction. "Don't push it, Cavanaugh," he warned, but Shayla could have sworn she detected a hint of a smile curving the corners of his lips.

He seemed to be coming around a great deal faster than she had anticipated he would, she thought. But then, she had never been around anyone who had so much room for growth and progress in his makeup.

Most people she had worked with only had to go from a D to an A. This man had a huge area for growth, going from the absolute last letter of the alphabet to the very first one.

"What are you grinning about?" Gabriel asked.

"Just glad we're working together and that things appear to be going so well."

Gabriel shook his head. "Maybe I shouldn't ask."

"Oh, but then you'd miss out on so much," she pointed out.

His eyes met hers. "My thoughts exactly."

"Admit it, I'm getting to you," she replied, smiling.

"Oh, I admit it all right," Gabriel answered, barely containing his temper. "I just have no idea what to take in order to combat the feelings that are being stirred up."

"Feelings?" she questioned. Was he saying what she thought he was saying?

"Like nausea," he supplied.

Gabriel expected his partner to take offense. Instead, she smiled at him, and then told him, "The detective doth protest too much."

"Uh-huh." The single annoyed word was meant to dismiss her, but no such luck. Instead, it just made her think of something else she needed to tell him.

"By the way, remember those parties I told you about? The ones my uncle Andrew likes to throw frequently and for no apparent reason?"

He remembered. "What about them?"

"He's throwing one in a couple of weeks."

He shrugged as he got back into his vehicle. "Good for him."

She continued watching his face as she got in on the passenger side. "And you're invited."

About to put his key into the ignition, Gabriel stopped dead. "Why?"

"Because you're my partner," she said simply.

That didn't seem like a good enough reason for anything, he thought, annoyed. What was it about this family that got under his skin like some sort of bad itching powder? All he wanted to do was be left alone and do his job.

"You know, I think it's time to dissolve this partnership," he told her.

"Too late," she said cheerfully. "I'm afraid you're stuck with me. At least for the time being." She pointed out the window. "The way's clear now. You can go at any time."

If only that were true, Cortland thought, turning on the car's ignition.

Chapter 16

"I have an idea," Shayla announced.

She and Gabriel had been working on the last two murders committed by the Moonlight Killer for the past two days, talking to as many people—hoping to find possible witnesses—as they could.

Sadly, they were getting absolutely nowhere.

They were back at the precinct now. Shayla had been going through the current mug shots on file, looking for a criminal who even vaguely resembled Cortland and the likeness that the precinct's sketch artist had drawn based on Josephine Juarez's description.

So far, Shayla hadn't been able to find anyone.

Caught up in the files he was going through, Gabriel took a few moments before he raised his eyes and looked at his partner. "Can't wait to hear this one," he murmured.

"You know, you could sound a little more support-ive," Shayla told him, although she knew it was useless pointing this out.

"This *is* me being supportive," Gabriel replied. "When I'm not being supportive, trust me, you'll know it."

Considering his sarcastic responses at times, that might prove rather difficult. "I'm not so sure about that," Shayla told him.

This back-and-forth was getting them nowhere, Ga-briel thought. "All right, what's this big idea of yours?"

"Well, I've gone through all the current perpetra-tors we have in the pages of these books," she told him, indicating the numerous volumes on her desk. "I was thinking that maybe our guy was never arrested in Or-ange County. Consequently," she extrapolated, "there might not *be* a current mug shot of him in our books. *But* there might be a current poster that we can·find in the mug shots of the criminals in Los Angeles."

Gabriel thought her words over and decided that she might actually have a point. "I suppose it's worth a shot."

Shayla smiled. "I'll take that as high praise," she quipped, then turned serious. "Do you know anyone back in your old squad room who we could call to get our hands on those mug shot books?"

Cortland shook his head. "Not really. Anyone I knew has either retired, transferred or, in one case, died."

They had hit another wall, she thought. Apparently

the people he worked with didn't exactly have an overly long work expectancy.

"That doesn't sound very helpful. Maybe, since you're my partner, I should make sure that my insurance is all up-to-date."

It occurred to him that although he knew she was part of the Cavanaugh family, he really didn't know any personal information about her.

"Why?" he asked, deciding this was as good a place as any to start. "Are you married?"

She looked at him in surprise. "No," she answered, thinking he'd already known that.

"But you have kids?" Again, it was a question, not an assumption.

"No." Shayla watched her partner, amused. "Is that your way of finding out if you can ask me out?"

"No," he responded defensively. There was a small part of him that felt she had hit a little too close to home. The moment that occurred to him, he immediately stripped the thought from his consciousness. "It's my way of finding out why you would want to carry life insurance if you're not married and don't have any kids."

She decided that his world had to be exceptionally narrow. "Maybe I want to leave something to my mother," she informed him, "not to mention that I'd also want to make sure that no one would have to put out money for my funeral expenses."

Gabriel shrugged. He saw no reason for elaborate funerals of any sort. "To my way of thinking, once you're dead, you're dead. What happens after that doesn't really matter," he concluded.

His wife's death—or, more accurately, her murder—must have really done a terrible number on him, she thought, aching for her partner. She could only imagine what he had gone through and was probably still going through to some degree. If she was going to find a way to bring this man around, Shayla thought, she really had her work cut out for her.

"Oh, it matters," she assured him with enthusiasm. "You might not think so, but it does."

He looked at her incredulously. "You're trying to tell me that my death matters," he asked, amazed.

"Absolutely," she responded with feeling.

"To whom?" he questioned, stunned, even though he knew he should just drop the whole matter and not get embroiled in a discussion. He had learned rather quickly that engaging in a verbal battle with this woman would not lead to a victory for him.

"I don't have a family," Gabriel told her. "To whom could my death possibly matter?"

Shayla never hesitated for a moment. "To me," she answered, then went on, "and to the people you work with."

Gabriel closed his eyes, searching for his fragmented patience. It didn't help any that it was growing late and they had been at this for hours.

"Give me a break." He wasn't prepared for what she said in response.

"I think *you* should give yourself a break," Shayla

told him. "Stop pushing people away so hard. Just drop those defenses of yours and let things happen."

She was going to go on like this until he could find a way to get her to stop, Gabriel thought. Taking out his cell phone, he put it on the desk in front of him.

"Let me see if I can get hold of someone and have them forward those mug shots," he said.

"Then you *do* know someone at your old precinct," she said.

"No, but I'll find someone," he answered, adding, "Anything to get you to stop talking endlessly."

She beamed at him, happy that she had managed to get him to come up with a possibility, even if it was strictly intended to get her to stop talking.

"Whatever it takes," Shayla told him cheerfully.

Gabriel made the call to his old precinct. He had to put up with being transferred a number of times—and disconnected once—but in the end, he managed to find someone who promised to get the photo books sent over to his office.

It struck Gabriel, as he hung up the phone, that he actually thought of this squad room as *his* office. He had never even thought of the LA office in those terms, he realized.

"The mug shots are being sent over," he informed Shayla.

"Are they being sent or couriered?" she questioned.

Gabriel knew what she was saying. That "sent" referred to a haphazard directive, while "couriered" implied a process that was safeguarded.

Rather than answer her question, Gabriel sighed inwardly and picked up the receiver, dialing the number again so he could speak to the person in LA again, appealing to that person to take care of the job for him.

Twenty minutes later, talked out, Gabriel hung up again.

It was done.

"Anything else you want, Princess?" Cortland asked. "Need a dragon slain or maybe a mountain climbed?"

"No, I'm fine," she told him brightly. And then she thought of something. "Did that person you talked to tell you when he was bringing the albums with the mug shots?"

"Tomorrow. Why?" he asked suspiciously, eyeing her. Was she going to have him drive into LA to pick them up himself in the interest of efficiency, not to mention making sure that the albums with the mug shot posters actually arrived safely?

But she surprised him.

"Well, if we don't have to wait for the mug shots to be brought over today, then, seeing what time it is, we're free to leave." She began to gather her things and lock up her desk. "Can I buy you a cup of coffee or a soft drink?"

He scrubbed his hand over his face as if to wipe away the sleepiness that had been descending over him. He needed to wake up.

"I'd rather have a drink," he commented.

She looked at him. Was the man slipping up? "I thought you weren't supposed to have those," she said.

"I'm not," he confirmed. "Doesn't mean I still can't want one."

"No," she agreed, "It doesn't. Tell you what, why don't you come to Malone's with me?"

"To the bar?" Gabriel questioned.

"Malone's also serves food," she reminded him. "Pretty good food at that. I brought you that steak sandwich from there." She watched his expression for some indication that he knew what she was referring to. With Cortland, it was really hard to tell.

Gabriel shrugged. "No, thanks, I'll pass."

"I don't think you should." She saw her partner staring at her as if she had just suggested that he needed to run around buck naked for his own good. "You need to get out, to do something besides eat and sleep serial killer," she pointed out.

His eyes washed over her dismissively. "I have you," he said darkly.

"Yes, you do, but you're getting fairly good at ignoring me. You need more input and more people," she told him. She saw him about to protest and quickly added, "Trust me, the more you interact with people, the more your brain cells get stimulated.

"Cases get solved because of the oddest things," she went on. "For instance, the Son of Sam, that serial killer who swore that this dog told him to kill people, was caught because of an outstanding traffic ticket."

"Now you want me to look into unpaid traffic tickets?" he asked, not certain exactly what she was driving at.

"No, wise guy," she told him with a sigh. "What I'm saying is that you never know when you might come across something that gets you thinking and might actually point you in the right direction."

"So you're saying that talking to the people at Malone's will wind up pointing me in the right direction?" he asked.

"No," she corrected, "going to Malone's will keep me from beating on you And maybe, just maybe, something that's said there might just get you thinking about other possibilities. Bottom line, Cortland, is that you need to get out, to socialize a little more. It'll get those rusting wheels in your head greased up and moving in the right direction."

"I'm not going to get you to stop until I agree to go to this Malone's, am I?" Cortland asked.

"Not agree," she corrected, not about to be placated by a few meaningless words. *"Go,"* Shayla emphasized.

She had lost him. Again. This was becoming an annoying habit of hers. "You want to run that by me again?"

"In simple terms, I am not backing off until you and I walk into Malone's together." She gave him the highlights of the evening: "You get something to eat, you say a few words, listen to a few more words and then I'll untie you."

"Untie?" Gabriel echoed, his brow furrowing.

"That was a joke, Cortland. If you can't tell the difference between that and a straight statement, you're worse off than I thought and you *really* need to get out more and mingle with people." She could see that her partner was really resisting her suggestion. "Give me forty-five minutes. Forty-five minutes there and then you can go home. I'll leave you alone."

"Does that mean you'll stop nagging me about your family's party or get-together or whatever you call it?" he asked.

She sighed. She should have known that would be his bargaining chip. "One thing at a time, Cortland."

"In other words, no," he guessed.

"No, in other words, one thing at a time," she repeated. "Right now, let's go to Malone's. And next Saturday, we'll see about my dragging you over to Uncle Andrew's house."

He thought that was rather an apt description for what she was threatening to do. "Dragging me might be the only way you'll succeed in getting me over to that event," he said.

Shayla gave it one more shot. "I know that you haven't had time to figure out all the family connections here, but I think you should take note of the fact that as well as being the former chief of police before he had to retire to take care for his family, Uncle Andrew is also Uncle Brian's big brother. And, in case you forgot, Uncle Brian is—"

"The chief of detectives, yes, I remember," Gabriel said impatiently.

She nodded, then continued, "And while Uncle Brian does not believe in throwing his weight around in any manner, shape or form, you might think twice before disrespecting his older brother by not coming to one of Uncle Andrew's gatherings that you've been invited to attend."

"Point taken," Gabriel answered, none too happily. Switching off his computer, he got up from his chair. Maybe if he faced the first battle, he'd be lucky and the second one would fade away. "You want to lead the way to Malone's?"

Her eyes were shining as she told him, "I would love to."

Chapter 17

Malone's was located a little more than a mile and a half away from the precinct. The reason Gabriel hadn't even noticed the friendly little establishment until now was because Malone's was a small, single-story building, only slightly larger than a yarn shop. Moreover, it was recessed from the middle of the block and, from a certain angle, appeared to be hidden.

At first glance, it was hard to say just where the front of Malone's actually was. Customer parking surrounded the rectangular building on three of its four sides, and most nights, the parking was far from adequate. Patrons had to leave their vehicles parked out on the street, either close by or somewhere in the immediate vicinity.

Shayla and her partner had arrived early enough to avail themselves of parking within the lot that surrounded Malone's rather than somewhere down the block—or farther.

"Looks like they're not all that busy," Gabriel commented, getting out of his car just as his partner walked up to him. He was looking around the parking lot just before he walked into Malone's.

There were a number of people inside, but it wasn't exactly crowded.

"It comes in waves," Shayla told him. "People on the force drop by for a little company, to exchange a few words, have a drink or two, maybe even get something to eat, and then they're gone."

It sounded like an experience that would be over before it even began. He couldn't see why it had been so important to her for him to come to the establishment.

"And why again am I here?" Gabriel asked. As far as he could see, this place looked singularly unimpressive.

That was simple enough for her to answer. "To get your feet wet socializing with your fellow police officers and detectives."

Gabriel looked at her as if she had lapsed into some sort of foreign tongue. Shayla tried again to explain what she was saying in as simple a language as she could.

"I think you need to get used to it. What you see here is nothing compared to Uncle Andrew's parties," she told him. "It's like comparing a World Series game to the first game being played at the beginning of a kindergartner's Little League season.

"At one of Uncle Andrew's gatherings, people don't come in shifts the way they do at Malone's. They stay for as long as they can. Not only that," she continued, "but they bring their wives, their husbands, their significant others and their children." She smiled, thinking about those gatherings. "And Uncle Andrew feeds all of them," she told her partner as she found two empty seats at the counter for them.

"And he feeds all of them," Gabriel repeated, stunned despite himself. "Isn't that a little pricey?" he asked, unable to imagine anyone wanting to voluntarily go to all that trouble and expense.

Shayla hadn't expected him to remember. "Like I mentioned before, the guests all contribute to the cost."

He frowned slightly. Whether or not he intended to turn up—and right now, he was leaning heavily toward "not"—Gabriel felt obligated to put in some money. Just because he wasn't going to attend didn't mean that the food intended for him didn't have to be paid for.

Taking out his wallet, Gabriel asked his partner, "How much?"

But she shook her head, stopping him before he could take out any money. "This is your first time. There's no need to pay until you turn up to at least a few of Uncle Andrew's gatherings."

"So, some people don't turn up after their first time?" Gabriel asked, pleased to be proven right.

She shot her partner down very quickly. "Hasn't been known to happen yet," she told him. "Don't worry, Uncle Andrew's gathering isn't happening for more than a week yet. There's plenty of time for you to get used to the idea."

Gabriel frowned. "Why does my showing up at your

uncle's house mean so much to you?" he asked. None of it made any sense to him, not turning up at the so-called family gathering or even here, at Malone's.

"Because I figure on some level, it'll actually mean something to you," Shayla told him. She smiled at her partner. "Think of it as a free lunch around your fellow police personnel. Free is always good, isn't it?" she asked, peering into his eyes.

"Not if I have to pay for it with my time," he answered.

Shayla blew out a breath, shaking her head. "You are a very stubborn man, Detective Gabriel Cortland. You are aware of that, aren't you?"

For the first time, she saw a small grin appear and slowly move over his face.

"Vaguely," he admitted.

The man behind the counter made his way over toward Shayla. He smiled at her. Sharp, blue-gray eyes took the measure of her companion.

"This your new partner, Shayla?" the gray-haired man asked.

"Yes, he is," she told the man. "Casey, let me introduce Detective Gabriel Cortland. Cortland, this is Sergeant Casey Buchanan, one of the sharpest men to ever retire from the Aurora police force."

Casey wiped his hand on his apron before offering it to Gabriel. "Hear you two are tracking down the former LA Moonlight Killer," Malone's newest owner said. "How's that going for you?" He looked from Shayla to Cortland.

Gabriel raised his brow as he glanced at Shayla. "Does everyone know?" he asked.

"First of all," his partner explained, "Everyone who walks through those doors talks to Casey. It's an occupational hazard. Casey knows *everything*. Second, like any police department, the Aurora Police Department is its own small, self-contained community. That's why I thought that coming here might just stimulate your thinking process. Get it moving in a different direction than it had been going previously."

Casey had always been able to read a situation and had become quite good at defusing possible explosions practically from day one. With a genial expression, the slightly heavyset man suggested, "Since this is your first time here, how about a drink on the house, Cortland? Your choice."

"Better yet, how about a hamburger on the house?" Shayla countered. "We've both put in a really long day, and Cortland's hungrier than he is thirsty," she told Casey.

The former sergeant nodded. "One hamburger coming up. You, too, Shayla?" he asked, looking at the young woman he had known since before the day she was christened.

Shayla smiled her answer. "You talked me into it, Casey."

"Knew I could." His gaze swept over the duo. "Be right back," he promised.

The moment he left, Gabriel regarded his partner. "And this—" he waved a hand around in general "—is supposed to stimulate my brain cells?" he questioned.

"Give it a chance, Cortland," Shayla counseled. "It's a process."

"If you say so," Gabriel muttered under his breath with a dismissive shrug.

"Hey, newly minted detective," a male voice called out by way of a greeting. Her oldest brother, Christian, came up to where Shayla and her partner were sitting. "I hear the lieutenant put you to work on the Moonlight Killer case." Christian nodded his dark head. "Impressive for your first time out, kid."

The detective turned to look at the man sitting next to his baby sister. "Hi, you must be her partner." Christian put his hand out toward Gabriel. He made a mental note to find out all he could about this new detective.

"I must be," Gabriel answered. After a beat, he shook the hand that was being offered to him.

"You have to forgive him," Shayla felt obligated to tell her brother. "People aren't all that friendly where he comes from."

Tickled, Christian laughed. "He'll learn. Being partnered with you, he'll have no choice." He glanced at his watch. "I've got to get going. I promised Suzie Q I'd be home in time to help put the kids to bed. If I hear anything about that serial killer, I'll be sure to pass it on."

Turning from Shayla, he glanced in Gabriel's direction and said, "Nice meeting you. And I'd remember to take my vitamins if I were you, Cortland. Your new partner is a tough woman to keep up with."

"Exactly what did your brother mean by that?" Gabriel asked after Christian had left.

Shayla raised and lowered her shoulders. "I haven't

the slightest idea," she answered—a little too innocently for Gabriel's liking.

Casey had just walked out of the kitchen carrying a tray with two hamburgers, each nestled in separate baskets and resting on top of a bed of French fries.

He had just set the tray down on the counter between them when each of their cell phones began to ring.

They all knew what that meant, including Casey.

"Take the baskets with you," he instructed. "You can bring them back the next time you come by."

"Cavanaugh," Shayla declared the second she brought the phone close to her face.

"Cortland," Gabriel said into his phone.

Both fell silent as the persons on the other end began rattling off information that made their blood run cold.

Gabriel listened closely to the directions he was being given. Both calls were over with in less than a minute.

Standing nearby, Casey read their faces and shook his head. "This guy can't stop himself, can he?" he asked as Shayla and her partner rose from the counter.

"That's why we have to, as quickly as humanly possible," Shayla told her late father's friend. She nodded at the basket that she was taking with her. "Put this on my tab, Casey," she said. "I'll catch you next time."

"Don't worry about it," the former sergeant told her, waving her words away. "Just get this SOB," he called after the two departing detectives.

"He's not taking a break," Shayla said in disgusted amazement as they walked out of the bar. "He used to let months go by, but now it hasn't even been twenty-four hours."

"Actually," Gabriel said just before he got into his car and took off, "I think this one was done before the other two."

Shayla found herself standing there, staring after the departing vehicle. What Cortland had just said left her totally in a daze. The person from the precinct who had gotten in contact with her hadn't given her any of those details. All she had been told was that another one of the Moonlight Killer's victims had been discovered in a freshly painted gas station bathroom.

It was supposed to be opened up tomorrow, but the attendant had decided to check the bathroom out first and to air it out as well. The gas station attendant had just peeped in to make sure that everything was as it should be in the single-stall bathroom before leaving for home.

Obviously, she thought, chewing her lower lip, it hadn't been.

Shayla got into her car and quickly drove to the gas station that was the scene of the latest gruesome discovery. Ironically, it was located less than a block away from another, almost identical gas station.

Given the close proximity between the two, what had made the killer choose one gas station above the other? Was it the victim he was stalking or the location that had drawn him in?

And why had Gabriel said that he thought this murder had been committed before the murders of the convenience store clerk and the master's degree candidate in the library stacks?

And, even more importantly than that, why had the killer upped his killing spree? she couldn't help wondering.

Was there a reason for it, or had the bloodlust just completely overwhelmed the killer, pushing him to kill even more victims faster than before?

There were so many questions involved here and so few answers, she thought.

The next moment she promised herself that she would find the answers as well as find the killer.

She had to believe that.

She was aware that some crimes were never solved, but those were usually single crimes with single victims, not crimes perpetrated by serial killers, because the more times the man—and sometimes the woman—ventured out to kill a victim, there was that much more of a chance that he would make a fatal mistake, one that would trip him up and lead to his capture.

Turning in to the gas station in question, she noted that there was a convenience store located almost right next to the gas station bathroom.

She wondered if there was some significance in that or if it was just a simple coincidence. From what she had read in the autopsy reports, which included where the murders had been committed, this was apparently only the second convenience store that was involved in the serial killer's spree. In the first convenience store, the victim had been hung from one of the sturdy shelves, then cut down by the killer.

In this one, according to the woman who had given her the information, the victim had been suspended from the bathroom stall.

As she drew closer to where the crime had been committed, she saw that once again, the crime scene investigative unit had arrived on the scene ahead of her. Given that they were driving a larger vehicle, one that they had to load up with all the items that were necessary to carefully document everything that happened at the crime scene, she was surprised to see the CSI vehicle there.

She was even more surprised, Shayla realized, to see that her partner had beaten her to the site as well.

The man didn't even know his way around Aurora yet—how the hell had he managed to get here first?

She had to give the detective his due, Shayla thought as she pulled her vehicle up next to his and parked it. He was obviously boning up on the city.

Chapter 18

Cortland was standing just inside the gas station bathroom, solemnly studying the victim. Dressed in pants and a soft, frilly blouse, the dark blonde had been hog-tied exactly like the other victims. This time the victim was suspended from a rope that was thrown over the top of the bathroom stall.

Shayla drew closer to her partner. He looked so deep in thought that, for a moment, she debated whether or not to say anything that might intrude.

Eventually, he snapped out of it, which was when she asked, "What did you mean by saying you thought that this victim wasn't the latest one?"

He rose to his feet. "Something the person who called me from the precinct said about the crime scene," he told Shayla. "That the bathroom had been remodeled and painted and then locked up for a couple of days to keep the public out while the paint dried.

"And then there's this," Gabriel said, pointing to the mirror just above the newly installed sink. Painted across the mirror in what appeared to be leftover beige paint were the words *Missed you, Det. Cortland* in large, bold letters.

Shayla's mouth dropped open. She had no idea how she could have missed that. She supposed that it was because her attention had been entirely drawn to the victim—and to Gabriel's reaction to the woman.

"He's made this purely personal," Shayla said, stunned.

"He made it personal when he went after my wife and killed her," Cortland corrected, doing his best to keep the hurtful words at bay.

She had noticed how carefully he had gone over the body. "Did you find another injection site on her?" Shayla asked.

He shook his head. "Not yet, but all that means is that he might have injected her through her clothes. Most likely, he snuck up on her, but I'm guessing she turned around and he had to make do with whatever area he could get to in order to inject her with the neuromuscular paralyzing agent," Gabriel said.

That made sense, she thought. Shayla looked around, trying to find someone on the CSI team. She wasn't necessarily looking for her uncle, but that was whom she spotted. Sean Cavanaugh was talking to another member of his team. She quickly made her way over to her uncle. She noticed that Gabriel followed in her wake.

For once, her uncle was not smiling. Nodding at the duo, Sean said grimly, "Looks like the serial killer upped his game. I'm not sure how much longer we can keep this out of the papers. The second this gets out, we're going to have a full-scale panic on our hands. This looks like it's personal," he said, echoing Shayla's words.

Because this sort of attention made her partner uncomfortable, Shayla answered for him. "Cortland was closing in on the killer back in Los Angeles," she explained, lowering her voice. "And then the Moonlight Killer did away with his wife."

She still wasn't sure how her partner managed to function. This sort of thing would have devastated so many other people.

Glancing toward Gabriel, who had stepped away for a moment, Sean nodded. "I am aware of the background details on the case," he told his niece. It was his way of telling her that there was no need to go any further with her explanation. "Obviously the serial killer found out that Gabriel had transferred to Aurora, and he had decided to bring his game out here to punish him.

"What amazes me," Sean continued, "is that the killer actually waited for your partner to dry out and get his act together before he resumed his gruesome spree."

"Maybe that's why he upped his count so quickly, to make up for the long break and lost time," Shayla said grimly. She watched her partner as he moved around just outside the bathroom. She didn't want him overhearing her ask her uncle, "Why do you think the killer feels so connected to Cortland?"

"That is anybody's guess," Sean told her seriously.

"Because he's a sick SOB and doesn't really need a reason for anything he does," Gabriel said as he rejoined the two inside the crime scene. Obviously, Gabriel had overheard despite his partner's precautions. "Personally, I don't care why he does what he does. I'm just interested in making him stop as soon as possible. I want to get this homicidal maniac off the streets, one way or another."

"Amen to that," Shayla agreed with feeling. "Do we have an approximate time of death for this woman yet?" she asked, turning toward her uncle.

"Not yet, I'm afraid. But we do have a name," Sean told her. "Her name is Gayle Parker, according to her driver's license."

Something struck her as being a little odd. "You notice that the serial killer never tries to hide his victims' identities?" Shayla asked her partner.

He had already thought about that. "My guess is that he's proud of his kills and wants everyone to know about them," Gabriel told her. "The faster his victim can be identified, the more people can be affected by her death. And the more people who are affected, the more gratified the Moonlight Killer feels."

Shayla frowned at the very idea. "Just what the county needs, a serial killer who's an overachiever." She looked at her uncle. "Has anyone been sent to notify her family or next of kin yet?"

"Not that I know of," Sean told her. "Her wallet was just turned up. Are you volunteering?"

"Not willingly," she admitted. "But someone has to

do it." As she said the words, she glanced in her partner's direction.

Gabriel knew what she was asking him, even if her lips weren't moving. He nodded. "I'll go with you."

She knew he didn't have to. It only took one person to do the notification. "I appreciate that," Shayla told him.

"We'll go in the same car," Gabriel told her, then surprised her by saying, "You drive."

She hadn't expected him to surrender the cherished male position of being the one behind the wheel. It had her wondering what was behind this. "Are you sure?" she questioned.

"No," Gabriel answered. "So let's go before I change my mind."

The site of the latest murder to be discovered, if not the actual latest murder to be committed, was in a parking lot that was adjacent to a much larger lot. That lot provided parking for a grocery store, a pharmacy and several stores that specialized in high-end clothing at low-end prices.

Leaving Gabriel's vehicle parked there posed no problem. What they were about to do, however, did.

The address on the driver's license was for a ground-floor apartment in a development of close to a hundred garden apartments.

Shayla pulled her vehicle up in guest parking closest to the apartment number she had. Considering the number of apartments in the immediate area, the available guest parking was sparse.

After getting out of her car, she waited for Gabriel to

do the same. "Apartment eighty-one is right over there," she said, pointing it out.

As they approached, she saw that there were lights on, "Let's get this over with," Gabriel said, leading the way to the apartment's front door.

It took three rings before anyone responded.

The front door flew open and an exasperated man of about thirty-five or so cried, "Where the hell have you been?" before he realized that he wasn't talking to the victim.

Alex Reynolds looked at the two people standing on his front step, holding official-looking shields.

"Sorry, I thought you were my girlfriend," he apologized. "She's been missing for three days and I've been worried sick. This just isn't like her."

Shayla took an inward breath and held up the victim's license for him to look at. "Is this her?"

"Yes!" he cried. And then he turned pale as he stared at the driver's license. "Where did you get that?" he asked fearfully, his eyes darting from Shayla to the man standing next to her.

"Mr. Reynolds, I'm afraid we have some bad news for you," Shayla began very quietly and respectfully.

The man's knees buckled. Had Gabriel not been standing right there to catch him, Reynolds would have wound up passing out on the floor in his doorway.

As it was, Gabriel caught the man and half carried him into the apartment he now lived in alone.

They wound up staying with the dead woman's boyfriend for close to an hour. Gabriel remained silent for the most part, with Shayla doing all the talking as well as doing what she could to comfort the bereaved man.

She discovered that Reynolds and the woman he had reported missing as soon as the missing persons department was able to take the information had planned to get married at the beginning of next year.

Shayla filed that bit of information away for later.

What she and Gabriel managed to do, once they got Reynolds to calm down a little, was question him about if there was anyone in Gayle's life that she was afraid of, or who might have followed her, wanting to harm her.

But Alex shook his head. The grief-stricken man couldn't think of anyone who would have wanted to harm his fiancée.

"Our life together was close to perfect," he told the two detectives, his voice breaking. "That's why, when she went missing, it just didn't seem like her. One of my friends said that maybe she just got cold feet, but she wouldn't have taken off like that. She would have come to me and talked things out. She certainly wouldn't have taken off and left her clothes behind," he insisted. "She just wouldn't have," Reynolds lamented as fresh tears came to his eyes.

In the end, Shayla called around to the distraught fiancé's friends and got several of them to come over and stay with Alex. She and Gabriel waited until the friends arrived.

"Sorry to make you wait," she told Gabriel as they walked out of the ground-floor apartment and to her car. "I should have had you take your own vehicle," she conceded.

Within moments, they were in her car and finally on their way back to where they had left his car.

"No reason to apologize," Gabriel told her. And then, after a beat, he looked at Shayla. He wasn't the kind to give compliments, but this had struck him at the time. "You were pretty good with that guy, breaking the news to him," Gabriel told her. "You seem to know just what to say, even though the poor guy must have felt like his very heart was being ripped right out of his chest."

It occurred to Shayla that that was a very concise description of what Reynolds had to have been going through.

But then, of course her partner would know all about that feeling.

"Was that how you felt?" Shayla asked him in a low, compassionate voice.

The moment the words were out of her mouth, she could feel her partner stiffening. She knew she had hit a nerve. Hit it hard.

But rather than make a denial or say something flip-pant or dismissive and change the subject, her partner actually answered her question.

"Yes. I felt like someone had stabbed me right in my heart. I kept hoping that it was all some sort of a nightmare, or that if I bargained hard enough, I would be the one who was dead and not Natalie." He sighed, vividly remembering the whole awful ordeal. "The pain grew so intolerable, I tried really hard to drown it, but I couldn't. For some reason, no matter how much I drank, I couldn't drown me, either. I'd always wind up passing out before I could drink myself to death," he said with a dark laugh.

"What made you decide to sober up and live?" she asked him, hoping that if she got him talking about his ordeal, he could finally begin to put it past him.

Gabriel stared at her for a long moment. No one had ever asked him that before, not even his old captain at the LA precinct. Captain Kelvin was just happy to sign the release documents, getting rid of someone who had once "been a really good detective," the man had said to him as his final parting words.

"Because I realized that I couldn't die before I avenged my wife and unborn baby, bringing that scum to justice." He knew that had to sound hokey, but he didn't care. That was how he felt. "And I realized that I couldn't do that if I was drinking, no matter how much I wanted to drown the pain I was feeling. So I stopped."

They had reached the parking lot where they had left Gabriel's vehicle earlier, and he looked at her.

For a second, the silence in her car was almost deafening. And then Gabriel finally spoke. "Any other questions?"

"Only how can I help?" Shayla asked.

"You're already doing it," he told her. She hadn't backed away from him, hadn't thrown her hands up and just walked away from the investigation. If anything, she kept at it just as intently as he had. Though he had initially complained that she was annoying, he realized now that her support meant a lot.

Shayla nodded. "Well, I intend to keep on doing it until we finally have a resolution," she told him. "My advice to you is to go home and get some rest, but I have a feeling that you have no intentions of listening to that, so I have an alternate suggestion."

"Which is?" he asked, curious despite the fact that he felt he should just tell her he'd see her later, get whatever sleep he could and return in a few hours.

"We've got cots set up at the precinct for people who pull all-nighters," she told him.

He had no idea where this was going, so he urged her to continue. "Go on."

"We go to the precinct with this new information and put down everything we know on one of those boards we use in the squad room. You know, the ones to try to find some sort of common denominator that threads through the cases."

"Other than the fact that so far, all the victims we found were under forty, what else is there?" he asked Shayla.

"There's that paralytic drug used on them and the fact that two of the victims were getting married in the coming year."

"So?"

"That's what we need to find out," she said. "So is that just a stray fact, or does it mean something? And if it does, what does it have to do with the other victims?"

His hand was on the door, opening it. It was obvious that she had gotten him thinking.

And then, just as he slipped out of the passenger side, Gabriel said, "I'll meet you in the precinct parking lot."

Victory! Shayla thought, doing her best not to smile too hard.

Chapter 19

Gabriel walked into the squad room. There were only a few people in there at this time of night, as opposed to the regular number of detectives and officers during the daytime.

"You looking for Shayla?" a redheaded detective near the back of the room asked. Gabriel vaguely recognized the man as someone his partner had introduced him on the first day. The woman had insisted on introducing him to a lot of people, he thought.

He seemed to recall that the man's name was Jeff Anderson or something along those lines.

"Anderson?" Gabriel asked, not altogether sure that he remembered the name correctly.

"That's me," the detective confirmed. "Shayla's in

the conference room. Said to send you in there once you got here."

"Conference room?" he repeated. What was she doing there? That was where suspects were usually brought in for interrogation. Had she found someone to question in the time it had taken him to get here? He had already sensed that she was an overachiever, but at the moment, he didn't know what to expect.

Gabriel walked into the large, windowless room with its single long table. Right now, there was not just one but two bulletin boards set up side by side against the back wall. Shayla was there, her back to him, busy taping up photographs of all the Moonlight Killer's victims, both in Los Angeles and Aurora.

Surveying the photographs, Gabriel stopped dead when he saw the picture of his wife just before the photographs of the latest three victims from Aurora.

"What are you doing?" he asked, his voice dark and demanding.

She had heard him come into the room and was ready for the confrontation.

Shayla gave him a simple answer: "Looking for any and all similarities between the victims."

He forced himself to turn away from Natalie's picture. Looking at it hurt too much. "What are you looking to find?"

"Hopefully, a reason why they were killed," she told him. "The one thing that put them in someone's path to be murdered."

"Something they had in common," he said. "You

mean like the two women who were going to be getting married sometime next year?"

They had already discussed this. Maybe Cortland was just looking for reaffirmation. "Yes, like that," she told him.

Gabriel walked over toward his wife's photograph. Other than her name and date of death, there was nothing posted beneath her name except for his.

"Natalie was already married," he pointed out.

Shayla could hear the pain in her partner's voice despite the fact that he was all but spitting the words out.

"Granted, Natalie is the exception," she agreed. "You already said that you felt the serial killer killed her to teach you a lesson. We need to find out what the other sixteen LA victims had in common—if anything." Shayla nodded at the stack of files on the table, the ones she had just brought in. "I had all the files on the previous victims sent over from Los Angeles. *Something* has to tie them together."

He looked at the stack of files. It wouldn't hurt to go through them a second or third time, he thought. There could be something in the files he had missed.

"Where do you want me to start?" Gabriel asked.

She was surprised that he was so easy to instruct. She had expected Cortland to fight her on this the way he had fought her on almost everything.

"Just pick a file, match it to the photograph on top of the bulletin board and start reading," she told him. "Make a note of *anything* that strikes you. Oh, and when you get tired and want to sack out, the cots are set up in the back room." She could see by his expression that he didn't know where that was. "When you walk out of here, turn left, not right. The room's right there in the middle of the hall."

He nodded, taking in the information. "You are a handy woman to have around," he murmured under his breath.

Picking up on his barely audible comment, Shayla's mouth curved. "I try," she answered, getting back to the file directly in front of her.

They spent another couple of hours going through about half the files between them. They wrote down everything and anything that appeared as if it might have possibilities on Post-it notes, which, in turn, they put up under the photographs of the corresponding victims.

As it turned out, only a few of the victims had been planning to get married the following year. And, reviewing the information about the brides-to-be, none of them were using the same wedding planners. Different wedding planners working out of different organizations had been recruited. The same went for the places where the receptions were to be held.

"Well, it *was* a decent idea," Gabriel told her when another victim's file proved not to contain anything about the victim getting married any time in the year after her death. He tossed the file back onto the stack on the table.

"Just because they don't have a future wedding in common doesn't mean that there isn't something else going on in their lives that brought them to the killer's attention."

Shayla set aside the file she had been looking through and sighed. "But right now, I'm just too tired to think. I'm going to go get some shut-eye."

He was surprised by that. "You're not going home?" After all, she didn't live that far from here.

"Not in this sleepy state I'm not," she told him. "I'm liable to fall asleep at the wheel and hit someone. And drinking coffee to wake up is out. It would be counterproductive at this point, and I'd wind up much too wired for this time of night."

Shayla rose, leaving the files behind and making her way to the door. "I'll just grab a catnap and be ready to go in about an hour or so," she told him.

With that, she left the room.

He stood there, staring up at the photographs spread out across the two bulletin boards.

Crossing back to the desk, Gabriel picked up another file and opened it. He thumbed through several of the pages. Then, dropping the file, he sighed.

He hated to admit it, even to himself, but the words on the page were beginning to get blurry. He was as tired as his partner had told him she was. Maybe even more.

Gabriel supposed that grabbing those forty winks or so wasn't such a bad idea.

Dimming the lights, Gabriel walked out of the conference room. It took him a minute to remember where Shayla had said that the back room with the cots was located. That was his first clue that he was *really* tired. He usually had no trouble remembering things.

Making his way to the back room, Gabriel tried the

doorknob on a whim. He had assumed that since she was in there, she would have locked the door for her own protection, making him have to knock to gain access.

But the door turned out to be unlocked. Turning the doorknob very slowly, he opened the door and saw that Shayla was lying on one of the cots up against the wall on the far side of the room.

His partner appeared to be asleep. He did his best to enter and make his way very quietly into the room. He chose a cot was closest to the door. Gabriel didn't like to be caught napping if someone entered the room, even if that person was most likely another police officer. The sound of the door opening would be enough to wake him.

Lying down on the cot, he stretched out very slowly and then sighed.

Who would have ever believed that he would wind up here like this, he thought. After his wife's murder, he had just assumed that he would have been resting— permanently—on a slab at the morgue by now, not on a cot behind a police conference room.

Well, he was here now, at least for the time being. He might as well make the best of it.

Gabriel promised himself that all he wanted to do was to catch a few minutes of sleep and then he'd be back at it again, going through the victims' files and searching for that one common thread that Cavanaugh insisted was what had brought the Moonlight Killer into those poor women's lives.

Just a few minutes, Gabriel told himself. That was all that he needed.

And then he'd be back at it full force.

He didn't remember closing his eyes.

If anyone had asked him about what happened, he would have easily sworn on a stack of Bibles that he had just intended to get a few minutes' rest.

That was all, just a few minutes.

"Wake up, sleepyhead."

Gabriel started, all but jumping up when he felt the hand on his shoulder, gently attempting to shake him into consciousness.

He found that he had to rise to the surface, pulling himself out of the deep disorientation that only seized a mind during those times when it had fallen into an all-absorbing, penetrating sleep.

Gabriel jackknifed up, bumping his head against the wall next to his cot.

"I wasn't asleep," Gabriel informed her curtly.

The smile on her face was skeptical. "Do you usually snore when you're awake?"

"I don't snore, either," he told her.

"All right," Shayla said gamely. "Just what would you call it?"

"Resting," he answered, swinging his legs off the bed and preparing to stand up.

She nodded as if taking in the information. "You were resting very soundly," she told him, amused. Apparently, admitting to something as human as needing to get some sleep was beneath some people, she thought.

Her eyes slid over her partner. He still looked a little tired, but she knew he would protest the assessment.

"Ready to get back to it?" she asked. "By the way, I ordered some breakfast."

"Breakfast?" he repeated, still feeling a wee bit disoriented.

She nodded. "You know, the most important meal of the day, etc., etc. I figured if I had it delivered, neither of us would have to take any time out to go pick it up." On her feet, she waited for him to get up and join her. "How do you feel about French toast?"

He thought over her question as he got to his feet. "I don't think I'm ready for any kind of a steady relationship with it, but it's not bad once in a while."

She rolled her eyes. He had a penchant of making some minor things sound almost bigger than life.

"Well, you have some waiting for you in the conference room," she told him, leading the way back.

"I didn't ask you to get me breakfast," he called after her.

"No, you didn't. I just figured you might be hungry. Pursuing a serial killer is hungry work," she told him, adding, "You know, you don't have to treat everything as if it was a challenge to your authority because most of the time, it's not." She smiled at him as they sat down at the conference table. "It could just be thoughtfulness."

"Sorry," he apologized, thinking how different the work atmosphere was here than it had been back in his old precinct. There everyone was too busy with their own cases to spare a few words of cheerful camaraderie and send them in anyone's direction. That was obviously not the case here.

"I'm not used to anyone caring if I ate or not," he told her.

"I see," she observed. "Well, here in Aurora, we don't just have a partner's back, we have his front, his insides and all the parts in between," she told him with a smile. A smile that, like it or not, was beginning to get to him. "Now eat," she told him, indicating the Styrofoam carton on the table in front of him.

He sighed as if what she had just told him to do was a hardship for him, but she noticed that Gabriel quickly disposed of the contents of the carton.

"Where's your breakfast?" Gabriel asked.

She nodded toward the wastebasket. A white container was peeking out of the top. "I already ate it."

They continued with what Shayla had come to think of as "the elimination game." They would take something that she had found in one of the folders and see if either one of them could find something similar in one or more of the other files.

Having nothing better to work with, Gabriel made a list of both similarities and differences between what Shayla had found in the victims' files.

Three hours later, Shayla sighed. "This is getting us nowhere," she complained.

"Yes, it is," Gabriel contradicted, surprising her. She looked at him quizzically, wondering if he was actually being positive.

"Come again?" she asked.

"I think that idea that the victims had to have something in common in order to attract the killer's attention is a good one. The trouble is that we haven't been able to find what that one thing is yet," Gabriel said. "Doesn't mean we won't."

She sat back in her chair and looked at him from top to bottom. "Who are you and what have you done with my partner?" she asked Cortland.

"Apparently, I think better on a full stomach," he said with a short laugh. "I also think we need to talk to some of the victims' next of kin. They might be able to enlighten us about some of their relatives' habits that didn't find their way into the files," he suggested, nodding at the files on his side of the table.

"That," Shayla said, impressed with his suggestion, "is an excellent idea." She looked at the folders, each, she thought sadly, representing a victim. "We've got a lot of people to choose from. Most of the victims had someone in their lives who might be able to tell us something that wasn't in these files," she said, her enthusiasm growing right before his eyes. "All we need is a hint to point us in the right direction.

"Tell you what," she continued, her mind racing, "before we throw ourselves into the heart of LA traffic, why don't I come up with a list of questions we can ask the victims' next of kin, see if we can get an idea of what interested the victim. You know, if they went to ball games, did volunteer work, belonged to unusual clubs, things like that," she told Gabriel, excited about this new avenue of possibilities. "Somewhere in that mixture is the answer we're looking for. But," she guessed, "we're not going to know it until we come face-to-face with it."

"Sounds like it's worth a try," he agreed. "Because so far nothing else is panning out."

"At least he appears to be taking a break from killing women," she said, thinking about the fact that there had been no reports of the killer striking in the last few hours.

"Either that," Gabriel said, "or he's getting ready to strike again."

She wrinkled her nose as she pulled over a legal pad, preparing to write the list of questions she had mentioned. "I could have done without that."

The unbidden thought that his partner looked cute wrinkling her nose like that flashed through Gabriel's mind before he could block it.

Where the hell had that come from? he silently demanded.

The idea of getting out and questioning people began to look better and better to him.

Chapter 20

"How do you not let it get to you?"

The question had come out of the blue. They had been at this for several hours now, questioning a number of victims' next of kin for information. Consequently, they had also been forced to witness the sadness that these questions stirred up within the family members they spoke to.

What the purpose of these questions were, Shayla had told her partner, was to get some sort of feeling for the kind of women these victims had been and how they, as opposed to other women, might have attracted the serial killer's attention.

There had to be some kind of common denominator amid these women that they could find.

Cortland had lapsed into silence since they had finished questioning the last person on their list. She wasn't altogether sure that she had actually heard him saying anything at all. Her thoughts had been busy ricocheting in her head, so that might have gotten in the way.

Taking a chance, she turned toward him and asked, "What?"

Gabriel blew out a breath and approached the subject from a different angle, because he was really curious what made this woman tick.

"Dealing with all the chaos and havoc that this sick individual has caused to the victims, to their families and friends, why would you even *want* to have a career that deals with something as revolting as that? And how are you even able to smile like that?" he asked, mystified how she could possibly keep going after seeing what had been done to the victims.

"Well, for one thing, I think of my job as preventing killers from getting away with what they'd done and, even more importantly, from killing more people.

"If it weren't for people like us, Gabriel, people like the Moonlight Killer would be free to continuing destroying lives and growing more and more bloodthirsty," she told him. "And I'm doing this to avenge Gayle and Shirley and Natalie and Amanda and all the other victims whose lives that hateful creature has snuffed out."

He understood all of that, but he was having trouble wrapping his mind around the fact that she seemed so upbeat.

"But the things you've seen," he said, "don't they ever haunt you?"

She compartmentalized, but she didn't think she could explain that properly to Gabriel, so instead, Shayla told him, "They would if I wasn't completely focused on doing something about it. And," she added— and to her, this was the important part—"luckily, I have a great family, all of whom know exactly what I'm dealing with and who somehow, miraculously, know just the right thing to say when I do hit a stumbling block and feel like I'm not able to go on."

She smiled at him. The smile was so bright, he caught himself thinking he could see it in the moonlight. "That's the good thing about having so many of my relatives working in the police department."

"Yeah, well I guess that does make you lucky in a way. I don't have that," he said grimly, staring out through the windshield at the road in front of him.

"You can," she told him softly.

He looked at her. His partner was babbling. She knew he had no family. "What are you talking about?"

She worded her answer very carefully and deliberately. "You can start by coming to Uncle Andrew's gathering."

"And they'll do what, adopt me?" he asked sarcastically.

"Not right away," Shayla told him in all seriousness. "But you can talk to them, tell them about the case we're working on. They can offer advice, and more than that, they can commiserate. I guarantee there'll be a number of them who have dealt with the same kind of thing, or at least something close to it. Sharing like experiences can help lighten the way you're feeling."

He spared her a stunned look. "You're serious," he realized.

Shayla smiled even though she knew he couldn't see her face. "Completely. It's been known to happen. More often than you'd think," she told him. She could feel him growing impatient with the conversation, so for now, she changed topic.

"It's getting late. Why don't we stop somewhere for dinner?" she suggested, then instantly changed her mind. "Better yet, why don't we go to my place and I'll make you dinner?"

"I don't feel like having eggs again," he said, remembering what she had offered to make for him the last time. He just assumed that was her entire menu.

"I make other things than breakfast," she told him, amused.

"Like what?" he challenged, thinking she probably couldn't come up with anything right away. She didn't strike him as being domestic, which was all right, given her choice of careers.

Shayla thought for a moment, not because she had no immediate answer but because she was trying to remember what she had in her refrigerator.

"How do you feel about chicken parmesan or pork chops?" she asked. "Either one is fast, simple and you don't have to worry about getting a food taster," she told him, her lips curving at the end of her sentence.

He frowned. "Sounds like a lot of trouble for you to go through."

Why would she even want to put herself out this way,

he wondered. The day she had put in was just as long as his had been, and she had to be tired, he reasoned.

"No, it's not," she contradicted. "You obviously don't cook much," she went on. Before her partner could demur further, she quickly said, "All right. That settles it, you're coming with me. No more arguing."

"I wasn't arguing," he protested.

"Certainly felt that way to me," Shayla told him. "But now that's all over with."

Gabriel was about to protest that they didn't have time for this, that he still had work to get to. But glancing at the clock on his dashboard, he realized that more time had gone by than he had initially thought. Somehow, amid all the questioning and driving they had done since they left the station earlier, the day had gotten away from him. It was actually past normal quitting time—and then some.

"Look," Gabriel began in an authoritative voice he assumed would put an end to all this, "you don't have to do this."

What he wanted to do was take her back to the station, where she could get her vehicle and go home, not take him to her place and feed him.

At least that was his plan.

It died a quick death.

"I don't *have* to do anything," Shayla informed him, then insisted, "I *want* to do this."

The woman was going to argue him to death. "Why?"

Shayla rolled her eyes and sighed. "Stop asking questions and just drive like a good little partner."

Offended, Gabriel was about to protest again, then decided that winning an argument with her just wasn't in the cards, at least not tonight.

Besides, now that he thought about it, he had to admit that he really was hungry. As far as he recalled, there was nothing in his refrigerator either to defrost or for him to make a weak stab at cooking. All he had was a quarter of a loaf of bread, and he wasn't inclined to stop to pick up something.

His partner, he thought grudgingly, had won the argument by default.

"Okay," he said, turning his car in the direction of her house.

Shayla was really tempted to say, "That's more like it," but she knew he wouldn't welcome her cavalier assessment. So she just kept quiet and smiled to herself.

It was slow going, but the man was definitely coming around.

"What can I do?" Gabriel asked once they walked in through her door.

A thought occurred to her, but it had nothing to do with being helpful, and she knew that in his present state of mind, he definitely wouldn't welcome it.

But for all his scowling, she really found the man to be attractive, she couldn't help thinking.

She pushed the thought onto the back burner. The really far back burner. If this partnership was going to work, she couldn't allow herself to think that way.

"Well, you can lock the door behind you and then sit down," she told him cheerfully.

"You don't want me to help out in some way?" he asked. He wasn't all that handy in the kitchen, but there had to be something he could do.

"Well, if it's not too taxing for you, you can talk," she told him.

They had talked off and on all day. Mostly about the case, but that was still talking, he reasoned.

"About what?" he asked.

Shayla shrugged. "About anything you want. The case, a program you watched recently that you liked—or hated—and why." She paused for a moment as she took the pork chops out of the refrigerator. "Or you can tell me about your wife."

She saw him look up sharply at her. "I think we've had our fill talking about the case today. And I don't watch TV," Gabriel told her. "And as for—"

He didn't get to finish, because what he had said just prior to that had caught her attention.

"You don't watch TV?" she questioned, surprised. She wasn't glued to her set, but she did turn it on for background noise when she was home alone. Everyone she knew watched TV programs at some point or other.

"No," he told her with finality. "I don't."

"Ever?" Shayla questioned. He sounded so definite about it, it surprised her.

The next moment, she found out why. "I don't own a TV."

"Oh. Well, that would explain why you don't watch it," she commented. "Can I ask why?"

He hovered over her as she began to prepare the pork chops, suddenly feeling too antsy to sit. "Because I deal with tragedy every day. I don't want to spend my night welcoming it into my home as well."

"There are other things to watch," she told him as the pork chops sizzled on the frying pan. "A whole wealth of things, actually. Comedies, old musicals, classic movies."

He shrugged his shoulders, dismissing all the choices she had come up with in one gesture. "Not interested."

She had the flame on high. Flipping the pork chops over, she was nearly done with them. She had two pork chops for each of them. While the food cooked, she tossed a bag of frozen vegetables into the microwave in an attempt to round out the meal.

"Did Natalie feel the same way?" she asked.

"She watched old movies. Made me watch them with her." He had gotten rid of the set after her death. He couldn't bear to turn it on. Watching it stirred up too many memories, as did everything else in his house. He'd walked away from all of it.

Gabriel looked at his partner accusingly. "Why do you keep bringing her up?"

The answer was simple. "Because that's how we keep people alive who we loved but are now gone. By talking about them. And because every time you or I mention her, you look like your gut had just been vivisected. Why is that?" she asked gently.

"Because I failed her. Because she's dead because of me." The words came tumbling out before he could stop them. "We went to school together, high school *and* college, and she could have had anyone she wanted. Anyone. But for some reason, she wanted me." Gabriel shook his head. "If she had married anyone else, she'd still be alive today," he insisted, feeling his throat closing up.

"You can't know that," Shayla insisted. "Life has a way of arranging itself when we're not looking and there's not much we can do about that. Tell me," she said, removing the frying pan from the cooktop and placing the pork chops on two plates, "was she happy with you?"

Cutting open the bag of mixed vegetables, she poured out the contents, dividing them between the two plates.

"Yeah, I guess. For the most part," he qualified as an afterthought, not sure of anything right now. All he was sure of was that she was gone and he wasn't.

Shayla sat down opposite her partner at her dining room table.

"Well, that's all anyone can ask for," she told him. To keep the somber mood from taking over, she asked Gabriel, "What would you like to drink?"

"A Black Russian," he answered without hesitating. Before she could say anything, he said, "But I'll settle for a soft drink."

Relieved, Shayla inclined her head. "One soft drink coming up."

"I can get it," Gabriel protested as she bounced up.

"I'm already up," she told him, going to the refrigerator and taking out a can. Rather than pour the contents into a glass, she placed the can next to his plate. "Tell you what, you can rough it and drink it straight out of the can."

"Wow," he said, pulling the tab, "makes me feel like a rebel."

Her eyes crinkled as she smiled at him. "Whatever works." She sat down opposite Gabriel again and began eating her dinner. "I hope the pork chops are to your liking. I made them to suit my taste," she confessed.

"They're fine," he told her. "Actually," Gabriel reconsidered his words, "better than fine."

She nodded, smiling at his assessment—and the fact that he had corrected himself. "Glad you like them."

Shayla watched as he made short work of the two pork chops on his plate. She hadn't seen him enjoy something to this extent and decided that he wasn't just paying her lip service.

She slowly consumed one of her pork chops and then waited until he was finished.

"Would you like another one?" she asked.

"That's your dinner," he protested.

"It's dinner," she corrected, leaving out the possessive pronoun. "To be shared any way I see fit. And I want you to have it." Her eyes crinkled again as her lips curved. "It's nice seeing you enjoy something."

Why her words suddenly made him think that what he really wanted to enjoy was her, not food, he really couldn't fathom. It wasn't that he didn't find her attractive. Heaven help him, he did. But just because a woman was attractive had never left an impression on him, not since he had first began going out with Natalie—and certainly not since she had been taken from him.

In his case, his relationship with Natalie had truly brought new meaning to the phrase "One-woman man."

And yet, all these stray thoughts kept popping up in his head, being brought to life by something Shayla said, or the way she looked at him—or the strange longing he had been experiencing of late.

Working with Shayla made him extremely conscious of the loneliness that had been his companion for the last nine months. Conscious of how very empty his life had become since he had held his wife's lifeless body in his arms.

But, by the same token, working with Shayla had managed to fill up all those empty spaces inside him as well as helping to give his life a new purpose.

As much as he hated to admit it, Shayla was sharp and kept him on his toes. In addition, she kept his mind going, and most of all, she kept alive his hope that despite the odds, he would be able to capture Natalie's killer and bring that fiend in so that the serial killer could face justice.

"Yeah," he finally said, nodding toward his plate and responding to her comment about seeing him finally enjoying something. "This wasn't half-bad."

Shayla widened her eyes and suddenly clutched at her heart. "Please, be still my poor little heart." And then she looked at Gabriel, amused. "I don't know if I can handle such a heady compliment."

Gabriel responded by throwing a balled-up napkin at her.

Chapter 21

Quite honestly, Gabriel didn't really know just what had possessed him to throw that napkin at Shayla. It was truly the first lighthearted moment he had experienced in over nine months and without thinking, he had just gone with it.

Caught by surprise, Shayla laughed, batting away the balled-up napkin.

She managed to hit him square in the face. But since it was simply a napkin, there was no impact, just laughter. The kind of laughter that represented a release of stored-up inner tension.

Gabriel caught Shayla by her waist as she pretended to wipe his face with the napkin. He went on to pull her onto his lap.

Still laughing, their eyes met, causing them to share what was definitely a very atypical moment.

Quite honestly, Gabriel hadn't thought his actions out any further than that. His next move hadn't even occurred to him until it materialized, seizing him.

Encompassing her.

The kiss surprised him no less than it surprised her.

The moment their lips touched, this overpowering aura of disbelief came over each of them.

Each, for reasons of their own, began to draw back. And then, for those same reasons, they just continued to lose themselves in what they had started.

Guilt instantly sprang up within him—momentarily threatening to undo him—but it was no match for the throbbing joy that flooded through all of him.

Lord, but he had missed this. Missed feeling this alive, he realized. Missed feeling as if he was being completely drenched in rays of sunshine.

Still holding Shayla on his lap, Gabriel put his hand to the back of her head, drawing her just a fraction closer to him.

Drawing in that exquisite sensation he felt being created inside him as well.

Shayla hadn't planned for this to happen. It just seemed like one thing followed another and suddenly, here she was, kissing Gabriel and feeling incredibly stimulated and aroused by the simple act.

And then, just like that, he was drawing back, just as she feared he would.

"I'm sorry," Gabriel told her, feeling he had allowed himself to get carried away. Somehow he had taken advantage of the situation—and of her—when he hadn't intended to.

Shayla's eyes met his. On some level, even though she hadn't known him for that long, she sensed—or thought she sensed—what Gabriel was feeling. She did her best to help him push his feelings of guilt aside.

Guilt of this nature was, in her opinion, counterproductive, if not actually destructive.

"I'm not," she told him, her voice sincere and hardly above a whisper.

And then she kissed him to show him that it was all right. That there were no hard feelings and that anything that happened between the two of them tonight had her stamp of approval.

The kiss seemed to go on for a very long time.

It grew more and more heated by the moment until the very sensation of desire seemed to surround them. It succeeded in pushing back the rest of the world and caused it to remain outside the very small, intense circle that was being created by just the two of them.

Gabriel rose then, his lips still sealed to hers.

Some part of him had every intention of taking his leave and going back to his apartment. But in order to do that, he needed to stop kissing her, and right now, the thought of doing that left him feeling bereft.

So instead, he picked Shayla up in his arms, ready to carry her to the ends of the earth—or at least into her bedroom.

He drew his mouth away from hers and said only a single word.

"Where…?"

Shayla pointed toward his left.

Brushing his lips against hers, Gabriel carried the woman who had created a fire in his veins to her bedroom.

Once inside the small, cozy room, he elbowed the door farther open so he could walk in without any bumping into any obstacles.

Still carrying Shayla, Gabriel brought her over to the queen-size bed and gingerly placed her down, handling her as gently, as if she was a snowflake, easily destroyed by the slightest wrong move.

Almost dazed, Gabriel drew his head back, looking at her, all sorts of half thoughts vying for space in his head.

"This isn't supposed to be happening," he told her, his voice thick with emotions.

"No doubts, no misgivings," Shayla warned him, gently gliding her hands along his face as if she was committing it to memory by virtue of touch alone. "If this wasn't supposed to be happening, it wouldn't be," she assured him. "But it is. So just go with it," Shayla counseled, planting an array of light kisses all along his face and his neck.

Gabriel discovered that he was unable to resist her. Unable to just get up on his own power and walk away from her. It was as if he had been placed in some horrid state of suspended animation, desperately trying to get back to the life that had been so savagely ripped away from him.

Except that this wasn't his wife.

And yet, he couldn't just walk away from Shayla.

Couldn't force himself to stop the wild, erratic and almost celebratory feelings that were racing through his system, rejoicing right now.

It was insane, he knew, but he just wanted this to continue.

Heaven help him, he had been so very empty inside for so long, it felt wondrous to feel alive again, even just a little while. Overwhelming to experience all these wonderful sensations that were shooting up and down his body, reminding him that he was a man capable of feeling a wealth of fantastic things.

It was wrong, he knew, but heaven forgive him, he wanted this woman. Not *any* woman, but *this* woman.

It had been an eternity since he had felt this way, Gabriel thought.

He had been convinced that he would never feel anything even close to this ever again. Convinced that, in all likelihood, he would never feel anything at all.

And yet, here he was, wanting to be with this woman. *Wanting* this woman.

Desire was heating his body, bringing it up to temperatures Gabriel could only vaguely remember having ever experienced before.

But this wasn't right, he suddenly insisted in the next moment.

It just wasn't.

As if his thoughts had suddenly transferred themselves into her mind, Shayla took his face in her hands and intensely delved into his green eyes.

"It's all right, Gabriel," she assured him in a whisper. "Natalie wouldn't want you suffering like this. She loved you and would want you to be happy, or at least to *try* to be happy."

And then she concluded her argument by pressing her lips against his.

At that very moment, it was as if something had been ripped open within him. Even if he had wanted to, he couldn't resist Shayla a second longer.

Unbuttoning his shirt, Gabriel never drew his lips away from hers. It was as if they were hermetically sealed to one another—and only growing more so.

Tossing his shirt aside, Gabriel went on to divest Shayla of her blouse.

Their clothing managed to disappear at lightning speed until they were both nude, both eager to run their hands over one another's bodies.

Both eager to create a network of warmly pressed kisses along their quivering, hot skin.

Shayla found herself enthusiastically responding to Gabriel. More than anything, she wanted to experience that wonderful, hot, ultimate sensation—and yet she was trying to force herself to slow down a little rather than go racing to the end goal and all that meant.

But it was hard to slow down when she felt her body vibrating and humming the way it was. Hard to slow down when she could feel the sensation building inside her and growing to almost overwhelming heights.

And then suddenly, there he was, looming over her. Gabriel stroked her body, creating more fires inside her as he parted her legs. And then, smiling into her eyes and moving with almost incredible gentleness, Gabriel entered her.

Shayla caught her breath, doing what she could to steady herself even as her heart began pounding wildly.

The pounding increased at the same time that his movement within her grew to ever greater, more intense heights.

Shayla dug her fingertips into his shoulders, holding on to him tightly as her anticipation of the final explosion within her grew to huge, overwhelming proportions.

And then it happened.

That final moment came, seizing them and rumbling through both of them.

And then it was over.

Shayla felt Gabriel sink against her as the moment slowly slipped away.

She could feel her smile filtering all through her, but the next moment, she wasn't thinking about that. She was concerned about how Gabriel would react when he finally found himself floating back down to earth.

Would he feel guilty about betraying the memory of his wife? Disappointed in himself for weakening and giving in this way?

Angry at her for having "led him astray"?

She wanted to be prepared to talk him out of any negative feelings he might be experiencing. She wasn't sure how to go about that, or even, possibly for the first time ever, how to read his expression.

Since she had been raised to always be as direct as possible by a mother who valued the truth above all else, Shayla turned toward Gabriel after he had moved off her, and she searched his face.

"Are you okay?" she asked.

She had caught him off guard. "I thought I was supposed to be the one who asked that."

"These are extenuating circumstances," she told him philosophically. "Besides, you're the one with the heavy weight on your shoulders, not me. So, are we okay? Is everything all right?" she pressed, her eyes holding his.

A half smile curved his mouth. Instead of answering her question, he said, "She would have liked you."

"Natalie?" Shayla guessed, her heart quickening. This had to be the ultimate compliment, she thought.

"Yeah," he affirmed. Without thinking, Gabriel slipped his arm around her shoulders and drew Shayla against him.

"Not that I'm not flattered," she quickly made clear, "but why?"

That was easy enough to answer. "Because you're trying to get me to move among the living instead of just curling up and dying by inches every day."

She thought over his explanation for a moment. "I can accept that," she told him with a smile. Turning in to Gabriel, she leaned her chin against his chest and searched his face. "So we're okay?" she asked him.

He kissed the top of her head. "We're okay," he told her.

And then he pressed another kiss against her hair. And another. He could feel the same stirrings begin to unfold within him that he had felt earlier, yearnings that were flowering and taking possession of him even more intensely than they had in the first place.

His arm tightening around her, Gabriel brought his mouth down to Shayla's, kissing her and unleashing the feelings he had thought had been completely spent just minutes ago.

Apparently not.

Her eyes were smiling at him when brought his mouth to hers. "What's so funny?" he heard himself asking.

"Not funny," she corrected. "Nice. Very, very nice."

"I'm not sure I understand," Gabriel replied.

She placed her fingertip against his lips. "You don't have to," she told him. "Just keep kissing me." Her eyes were shining. "It'll come to you," she promised.

He shook his head, stifling what felt like the beginning of laugh.

He didn't feel like thinking right now. Feeling had so much more going for it. Gabriel opted for that.

Gabriel expected to wake up and find her still in bed next to him. He wasn't quite sure how to deal with that, waking up beside a woman. He hadn't done that since Natalie had been taken from him.

But as it turned out, he didn't have to deal with that. When he woke up, the place beside him was empty.

His mind racing, Gabriel grabbed his pants and pulled them on. He was about to hurry out into the hall when Shayla walked in, dressed and smelling of shampoo and some sort of enticing body soap.

"Hi," she said. "You can shower here and then go get a change of clothes at your place. I've already showered."

"I can tell." What she had used smelled enticing, but

it was definitely not meant for a man. "That the only soap you have?" he asked.

She paused to think. "Well, I have dishwashing liquid and also detergent."

"So in other words, no," he translated. "I'll shower at my own place, thanks."

"Okay, have it your way," she told him. "But before you do that, drop me off at the precinct."

He didn't quite follow her. "Why?"

"Because my car's in the precinct parking lot," she reminded him.

He thought for a moment, reconstructing his agenda. "Okay, change of plans. I'll shower here, then go to my place, and then we can go to the precinct so we can get back to work."

She saw no reason to argue with that and had just agreed when both of their phones began to ring.

Shayla felt her stomach sink.

Another murder?

She tried to think positive thoughts even as she said, "I think your shower might have just been put on hold."

With that, Shayla went to answer her phone. Out of the corner of her eye, she saw Gabriel trying to track down his cell phone, following the sound of ringing.

His expression looked far from happy.

Chapter 22

"I'm sorry, is this too early to call you?" the woman's voice on the other end of Shayla's cell phone asked apologetically. The next moment, the caller seemed to realize that she hadn't even identified herself yet. "Oh, this is Rose D'Angelo. You and that other detective came to my house yesterday and asked me questions about my sister, Cynthia Wells. You told me that if I thought of anything else about Cyndie, I should give you a call."

Shayla breathed a quiet sigh of relief. At least this wasn't about another serial killer victim.

"And you thought of something else," Shayla guessed.

She heard the woman on the other end of the call hesitate. "Well, I don't know if this means anything," she qualified slowly.

Shayla sat down on the edge of her bed. She could see Gabriel, on his own cell phone, watching her.

"Trust me, Rose, the smallest thing could lead to solving a crime. What did you remember?" she asked.

"It's something that Cyndie said to me about a week before she was killed."

"Go on. I'm listening, Rose," she coaxed. She saw that Gabriel was still looking at her, his body language asking if this was going anywhere. All she could so was raise her shoulders in a noncommittal shrug.

"Well, like I said, this is probably nothing," the woman repeated before telling Shayla, "Cyndie complained to me about her pharmacist. She said he was kind of creepy, to the point that she was thinking of changing pharmacies. I'm probably just reading things into that."

Maybe, maybe not, Shayla thought. "Would you happen to know this pharmacist's name, or the name of the pharmacy where your sister went to fill her prescriptions?" She crossed her fingers as she asked the question.

"I think she said his name was Stewart. The thing that struck my sister as kind of funny is that he told her he used to work in LA, but he liked the homey feel of Aurora better. He claimed it suited him, but it just made her feel really uncomfortable.

"And she left one of her prescriptions at my house, so I can give you the name of the pharmacy," Rose told her, then quickly added, "Don't get the wrong idea. Cyndie wasn't a pill popper or anything. She just gets—got," Rose corrected herself, her voice cracking for a moment.

Shayla quietly waited for the woman to continue. "She *used* to get these awful migraine headaches that would all but stop her in her tracks."

This had all the signs of going on for a while, Shayla thought.

"Rose, why don't my partner and I come over to your place so we can continue this in person?" Shayla suggested.

"If you don't mind, I'd rather come down to the police station." The woman paused for a moment, then explained, "It's a matter of closure, I suppose."

"Of course," Shayla told her. "Whatever works for you. My partner and I can be at the precinct in about twenty minutes," she promised, giving the woman the exact address. "Will that be enough time for you to get there?"

"Yes, I think so," Rose D'Angelo answered. "I'll meet you there." The woman sounded excited and hopeful as she terminated the phone call.

Shayla put her phone away. Gabriel had already put his own phone in his pocket.

"Anything?" Gabriel asked, trying to read her expression.

"Hard to say. Maybe," Shayla qualified. "That was a victim's sister calling. What she told me would explain how the killer got his hands on the drugs he injected into his victims."

She had definitely aroused his interested. "Go ahead," Gabriel told her.

"Rose D'Angelo said that her sister told her that her pharmacist made her feel really uncomfortable. She said the victim was actually thinking about changing pharmacies so she wouldn't have to interact with him."

"This could be promising," Gabriel said.

Shayla nodded. "The woman is coming in with the guy's name and the name of the pharmacy he works for. Oh, and one other thing she said," she remembered.

Whatever it was, it obviously had to have left an impression on his partner, or she wouldn't have felt it was important enough to mention, he thought.

"And that was?" he asked.

"According to Rose D'Angelo, her sister said that the pharmacist told her that he used to work in Los Angeles, but he liked the 'homey feel' of Aurora better." Shayla raised her eyes to his. "I'm trying not to let myself get too excited."

A half smile curved his mouth. "We can save that for later," he told her, thinking of last night and how surprised he had been by what had happened and his own reaction to it. "But this definitely looks promising."

"That it does," she agreed wholeheartedly. "What was your phone call about?" she asked as she quickly retrieved her shoes from under her bed and slipped them on.

Gabriel smiled. "It was from someone I used to work with a couple of years ago."

"I thought you said you no longer knew anyone there," she reminded him. Obviously he had stretched the truth.

"Yeah, well, I forgot. Anyway," he continued, "Diego heard I was looking to find out if one of the wanted posters in the LA precinct was of someone who resembled me. Diego got it into his head to look through them late yesterday." It was the kind of thing that would have tickled the detective, Gabriel recalled.

"Diego got the biggest kick when he found one. The guy's getting on in years," Gabriel confided, "and not exactly tech savvy, but he's going to get one of the other guys who works there to scan the wanted poster and send it to me. The poster isn't about a current case— it's about eight or nine years old—but Diego swears the person he found could have been my twin."

"And where is this twin now?" Shayla asked.

Gabriel shook his head. "No clue," he answered. "According to what Diego said, the guy was never located."

This was getting more interesting, Shayla thought. "Sounds like it might be another piece of the puzzle."

"Or it could be just a coincidence—or nothing," Gabriel pointed out.

"Your optimism is really overwhelming."

"I've learned to be cautious," he reminded her.

Shayla's mouth curved. "Me, I thrive on optimism," she told him needlessly. "It gives me the energy I need to keep going."

"To each his own," Gabriel said philosophically.

"My sentiments exactly," she said, her smile widening. "Okay." She rose to her feet. "Let's go, Gabriel— unless you want to take that shower first," she told him, giving him a choice. "I can call Rose back and tell her that we'll be a little late getting to the squad room."

"I can grab a quick shower at the precinct once we get our hands on the information she's bringing. Besides, Diego is going to have someone email me that wanted poster," he reminded Shayla. "I'm curious to see if this guy really does look like me."

"He might resemble you," Shayla allowed, "but I'm sure that you're far better-looking."

"A compliment?" Gabriel questioned, looking at her.

"Don't looked so surprised, partner. You must have a mirror somewhere in your apartment, right? You know what you look like."

"Yeah," he answered dismissively. "I know exactly what I look like—like that serial killer's worst enemy."

She nodded, going with the change in subject as they left her house. "We'll get him. We're getting close. I can feel it, Gabe."

Shayla was surprised to see his expression suddenly change. Was that pain she saw in his eyes?

"What's the matter?" she asked.

"Natalie used to call me that. Gabe," he told her.

The last thing she wanted to do was stir up any painful memories for him, especially after last night. Last night had given her hope that he was actually moving on.

"Would you rather I didn't?" she asked.

He thought for a moment, then reminded himself what Shayla had said—that Natalie would have wanted him to move on. And she was right. "No, that's okay. It just caught me by surprise, that's all," he admitted.

Still, Shayla thought, she would refrain from using the nickname, at least for now. They had already taken a huge step forward, and she didn't want to mess that up by insisting on using the shortened form of his name. It really wasn't worth it.

She could save that for a later date.

Provided, she qualified, there *was* a later date.

They managed to get to the precinct approximately ten minutes before Rose D'Angelo arrived. Gabriel parked his vehicle several spaces away from where Shayla had left her car the day before. It was early, but judging from the number of cars in the lot, it looked like it was going to be a busy day.

"Think she's here yet?" Gabriel asked, getting out and looking at Shayla over the roof of his vehicle.

"Rose D'Angelo is coming in from Mission Viejo, so I don't think so—not unless she wanted to get a speeding ticket."

"Mission Viejo," Gabriel repeated, trying to remember how far away that was from the precinct. They had interviewed a number of people yesterday, and he was still trying to get the lay of the land. "I've really got to start memorizing the names of the different cities and just where they're located around here."

"It'll all fall into place for you eventually," she promised him. "For now, let's just go in. I'm dying to see if that friend of yours found someone to help him send you that wanted poster. It would be interesting to find out if Josephine was just hallucinating or if she was actually right about bumping into someone she thought looked like you."

They got into the elevator. Gabriel frowned slightly. "Maybe I should start wearing a disclaimer on my jacket that says, 'Sorry, I'm not the serial killer you're looking for.'"

Shayla didn't find his comment the least bit amusing. "You know, that just gives us more reason to find this Moonlight Killer, because if you actually *do* resemble him, someone might just get it into their head to bring you in—or even worse, shoot you."

"Now who's letting their imagination run away with them?" he asked pointedly, glancing at her as they got off the elevator and headed toward the squad room.

She supposed he was right, but that didn't stop her from worrying. Out loud, she agreed, "One step at a time."

Rose D'Angelo arrived shortly after they did. Shayla was immediately on her feet, escorting the woman into the office along with Gabriel. She watched the woman's reaction as she came into the squad room, but Rose didn't appear to be unduly nervous. As a matter of fact, the victim's sister looked rather hopeful.

Shayla brought the woman to her desk. "Take a seat," she encouraged, indicating the chair next to her desk. Gabriel brought his own chair over.

Before sitting down, Rose took out and placed a half-filled prescription bottle on Shayla's desk.

"Oh, and Cynthia told me the guy's name was Stewart," Rose told her.

Rose had already told her that when she called, Shayla thought. Before she could say anything, though, Gabriel asked the woman, "Did she happen to know or hear his last name?"

Rose shook her head. "If she knew it, she never mentioned it. Like I told Detective Cavanaugh when I called this morning, Cyndie said she intended to change pharmacies, or at least go to another branch so she wouldn't have to run into him. She sounded pretty adamant about it, and my sister wasn't the kind who scared easily, so there had to be something to this, don't you think?" she asked, looking from one detective to the other.

"How long before she was killed did she tell you she was going to change pharmacies?" Gabriel asked.

Rose thought for a moment. "A couple of weeks, I think," she finally answered. The woman's breathing became a little more pronounced. Her expression was a combination of anger and fear. "Do you think he was the one who killed my sister and all those other women?"

"That would be jumping to conclusions," Gabriel answered, his voice almost deadly calm. "We're going to have to check some things out first."

"But you will tell me once you know, won't you?" Rose pressed. "You have to tell me," she insisted.

Gabriel nodded. "You have our word on it," he promised.

Rose D'Angelo remained in the squad room, answering a few more question dealing with her late sister, and then she left.

"So what do you think?" Shayla asked her partner the moment the woman walked out of the squad room. "Do you think this Stewart person is just a weird guy— or the Moonlight Killer?"

"Being a pharmacist would explain his being able to get his hands on the drug that he used to inject into his victims. At the very least, we have to track him down, This is possibly the first real lead we've gotten. The first order of business is to find out his last name and then get as much information on him as we can," Gabriel said.

"He could just be a creep," Shayla reminded her partner. "*Or* he could turn out to be *our* creep. By the way," she said as she grabbed her shoulder bag and rose from her desk, "did you get a chance to look at that wanted poster from your friend?"

He had forgotten all about that when Mrs. D'Angelo had walked in. Moving over to his desk, he tuned his computer on and scrolled through one message after another.

"This thing takes forever to warm up," he complained.

"Ah, but the anticipation makes the end product all worth it," she joked.

Gabriel leveled a look at her. "You know, Cavanaugh, if this job doesn't work out for you, you could always get one doing voiceovers for corny movies."

So, they were back to "Cavanaugh" again, she thought. Was that because the effects of last night were already beginning to fade away, or because they were at work and he felt more comfortable maintaining a distance between them here?

She decided that whatever worked for him was fine with her.

Shayla looked over at his screen, waiting for the details of the wanted poster to materialize. "You know, once we get a free moment, I'm going to request a new computer for you. You can get old waiting for this to warm up and give you a clear picture."

"Tell me about it," he muttered.

And then the screen began to grow clearer as an image finally formed.

The second it did, Shayla looked at it more closely, and then her mouth dropped open. "My Lord, it *does* look like you," she cried as she stared at the screen.

The more she looked at it, the more similar it seemed. It was, Shayla decided, positively eerie.

Chapter 23

Shayla looked away from the computer screen and at the man standing next to her. Granted, it looked like an old shot from his late teen years, but the resemblance was rather unnerving.

"You don't have any brothers or male cousins?" she asked Gabriel.

"I don't have *any* family," he told her. "The second I graduated high school, my mother took off with her then boyfriend. That woman changed boyfriends like most women changed clothes," he added. "I haven't seen or heard from her since. I figured she found someone to pay her bills. As for any siblings or cousins, male *or* female, that's a no."

Shayla turned so that her back was to the others in the squad room and no one would overhear them.

"How do you *know* there was no family?" she questioned. To her way of thinking, he only had his mother's word that there were no other relatives floating around.

"Trust me, if there was any family at all, my mother would have been on their doorstep with her hand out. She would have had me dressed in my oldest clothes and holding me in front of her to generate empathy as well as sympathy for her." Gabriel looked closer at the wanted poster on his monitor. "It says here that the guy's name is Howard Stewart. He was wanted for assaulting a woman nine years ago." He looked at his partner. "According to this, they're still looking for him."

"Send a copy of that to your phone—in case we need it," she told him. Picking up the prescription bottle Rose had brought to them, Shayla glanced at the address on it, then tucked it into her shoulder bag. "Let's see if we can get any information on that creepy pharmacist," she said as she walked out of the squad room.

"Information," Gabriel repeated. "You mean like his name?"

Shayla nodded. "That would be a good place to start."

The branch of Good Health Pharmacy that Cynthia Wells had frequented before her untimely death was a large, modern-looking pharmacy that, unlike some of its other branches, was open twenty-four hours a day.

When Shayla and Gabriel walked in and approached the rear counter, they found that there were two pharmacists currently on duty, both women in their forties. There was also a clerk to ring up the sales, as well as a young man who looked like he was still in college.

They began by showing their shields and IDs to the first pharmacist they saw, and Shayla requested to speak to the person in charge.

"That would be me," the woman told them. She was somewhat tired-looking, with short, dark blond hair. The name tag she wore proclaimed her name to be Christine Madison. "What can I do for you, Detectives?"

Without thinking, Shayla took the lead. "Do you have a pharmacist who works here by the name of Stewart?" she asked.

"You mean Stewart Howard?" Christine asked. "He's not here right now. He's working the night shift this week." Her curiosity stirred, the woman looked from Shayla to her partner. "What's this about?"

"We'd just like to ask him a few questions," Shayla replied, deliberately not being specific.

Listening in, the other woman behind the counter laughed shortly. "Careful what you wish for," she told Shayla.

Gabriel's attention was instantly piqued. "What do you mean by that?"

The other pharmacist—Kim Jordan, according to her name tag—came over to join them at the counter. "Well, nothing, if you're the one who's asking the questions," she told Gabriel. "But if your partner's the one doing the asking, and if he takes a shine to her, that man can go on and on. And *on*," Kim emphasized.

"Kim," Christine said sharply, looking far from pleased by Kim's comment.

Unperturbed, the other woman merely shrugged.

"Just letting them know what they're in for, Christine," she said.

"This Stewart person talks a lot?" Shayla asked Kim.

"Depends if you're a male or a female," Kim answered. When her boss gave her a censoring look, Kim withdrew. "Excuse me, I've got a lot of prescriptions to fill," she told the detectives.

"Don't mind her," Christine told them. "She and Stewart got into it the other day and Kim is the type to carry a grudge, but they're both good workers. Especially Stewart. I can always count on him to take the night shift without any complaints, which is more than I can say for some of the others here," she added without bothering to lower her voice.

"Do you have an address on file for this dependable pharmacist?" Gabriel asked.

The head pharmacist appeared rather taken with Gabriel, but not so much that she was about to rush off and give up the employee's address without asking any questions.

She glanced from one detective to the other, clearly debating the situation. "What did you say you wanted with him?"

Gabriel was ready with an acceptable excuse. "He was an eyewitness to a car accident earlier today. We just needed to ask him a few more questions, get the sequence of events straightened out," he explained.

Christine nodded and then pulled up the necessary information on her computer. "I guess that makes it all right," she said more to herself than to the sexy detective standing before her. She wrote the information that came up on the monitor down on a pad, tore off the sheet and then offered it to the tall, handsome man on the other side of the counter. "There you go."

Gabriel smiled his thanks and tucked the single sheet into his jacket pocket. "You've been very helpful."

The woman all but preened in response. "My pleasure, Detective. Please don't hesitate to come back if I can be of help to you in any other way," the woman called after Gabriel as he and Shayla walked away and headed out of the store.

"I had no idea you would turn out to be such a secret weapon," Shayla told him.

"What are you talking about?" he asked as he led the way to his vehicle parked at the curb.

Getting in on the passenger side, Shayla pretended to bat her eyelashes at him. "Oh, I think you can figure it out. Hey, I'm not complaining," she laughed as she saw Gabriel frown. "Christine was putty in your hands and gave up the guy's address without making us jump through hoops or get a court order—and she could have," she reminded her partner. "On top of that, you were so charming, we won't have to worry about her calling Stewart to warn him that he might be getting some unexpected visitors."

Pleased at how things had gone, Shayla shifted in her seat and smiled at him. "We make a pretty good team."

He didn't bother arguing. "Okay, partner," Gabriel said. "Now what? You want to see if this Stewart guy is home? If he's not, we could wait outside his place for him to come back."

"Now that we have the guy's current last name, we

can track down his license plate number through the DMV and find out the make and model of his vehicle. With any luck, we can get hold of his cell phone number as well so we can see if he's mobile right now."

Starting his car, Gabriel decided it would be prudent to drive over to the pharmacist's residence while they focused on tracking down the rest of the information they needed.

He did have one question for Shayla. "What do you mean by his *current* last name?" he asked.

"Didn't you notice that the order of the names were reversed?" she asked him. She could see by the look on his face he had no idea what she was talking about. "That guy on the wanted poster your friend sent over, his name was Howard Stewart…" She let her voice trail off as she waited for her words to sink in.

Gabriel felt like an idiot. He had been so caught up with the rest of it that this one glaring detail had managed to escape him. "The guy we're trying to find now is Stewart Howard."

"Could be a coincidence," she said. The last thing she wanted was to cause him to beat himself up over this.

The look on Gabriel's face told her he saw right through her attempt. "You know as well as I do that that would be one hell of a coincidence," he told her. Gabriel looked totally disgusted by his oversight as well as by the man they were looking to speak to. "That guy is just too full of himself."

"I guess that getting away with twenty murders, possibly more, just filled him with much too much confidence," she said. "Okay, let's drive over to our egomaniac's residence and I'll see if I can get those missing pieces of information we need to catch this guy," Shayla told her partner.

It turned out that their suspect lived in a small house, which he was currently renting from a retired couple who had recently moved to Florida.

Shayla called Valri to get the rest of the information they needed.

"I can't talk right now, Shayla. I'm really busy," Valri said when she finally answered her phone. "More so than usual."

Shayla interrupted her cousin. "I wouldn't ask you if this wasn't an emergency, Valri."

"With you they're *all* emergencies, Shayla," Valri said wearily.

"This is an *emergency* emergency," Shayla emphasized, talking quickly. "I think Gabriel and I might have found the Moonlight Killer."

There was momentary silence on the other end of the call, and then Valri urged, "Go on."

Shayla gave her a very quick summary about the pharmacist they were looking for, concluding with, "I need to know what kind of car he's driving and his license plate number. And if you have any cell phone listing for him I can track, that would really be the icing on the cake."

Valri sighed. "No promises, but I'll see what I can come up with."

"Cortland and I are sitting outside the guy's house right now," Shayla said by way of an added detail. "If you can come up with that information, I'll owe you my firstborn."

"By my calculations, you owe me your first twelve born," Valri told her cousin. "But I'll consider your tab closed for another steak sandwich from Malone's."

"You got it," Shayla promised excitedly, happy to comply. She closed her phone.

"So?" Gabriel asked, looking at her.

"She's looking into it and will call us back when she comes up with something," she told her partner. "Meanwhile, I suggest we call the lieutenant, tell him what we've found out so far and then get comfortable. I've got a feeling we might be here for a while."

He sighed. "My favorite part of the job," he muttered. "A stakeout." Gabriel shook his head. "Fastest way known to man to develop stiff joints," he complained.

"Well, there's no rule that says we both have to stay here," Shayla pointed out. "You can call for a cab and go back to the station."

"I could," he agreed. "The only trouble is, this is my car."

"I won't steal it," she promised innocently. Shifting in her seat, Shayla dug into her pocket and pulled out a set of car keys. "I'll even give you the keys to my car, and you can use them to drive yourself home once you get to the station and quitting time comes."

"Yeah, right," he said, dismissing her suggestion.

"Well, you can," she told him.

"Shut up, Cavanaugh. You'll make this a whole lot easier on both of us if you don't talk for a while."

Shayla stared at him, not sure whether or not to believe him. "Are you serious?" she asked Gabriel.

"No," he answered with a sigh. "I'm not. At this point, I'd probably find the silence deafening. But I do think you should call the lieutenant to let him know what we've decided to do at this point."

"It might sound better coming from you," she told him.

He shrugged. "Okay." Taking out his phone, Gabriel stepped out of the vehicle.

Gabriel had no sooner concluded his call to their commander and opened the driver's side door to get back in than Shayla's phone rang. Her body language when she answered the phone told him that the call was the one she had been waiting for, undoubtedly supplying the missing—or at least some of the missing—information that they needed.

Deciding the hell with privacy at this point, since Shayla would tell him about the call soon enough, he got back into the car.

Shayla's cousin slowly enunciated the license number before saying, "He owns a 2021 silver BMW sedan."

"That's not exactly an inconspicuous car," Shayla commented. Nor was it inexpensive. Where was he getting the money?

"A BMW does stand out," Valri agreed. "But silver blends in. That's the color of over a third of the cars out on the road, so it's a tossup," the computer expert said. "But the good news is that it's the latest model, so while I don't have a cell phone number for you to track, you *can* track his vehicle—and the better news is he's parked in his garage right now, so you can go and question him."

"Thanks, Valri. I owe you," Shayla said.

"Yes," Valri answered, "you certainly do. Good luck."

"Thanks," Shayla said as she terminated the call.

"Well?" Gabriel asked the second she lowered the cell phone.

Her eyes met his. "You'd better get some supplies," she told him, nodding toward the convenience store on the corner that they had passed on the way to the residential complex. "We both know that bringing in Stewart Howard—or Howard Stewart, or whatever he chooses to call himself—for questioning without any real evidence isn't going to get us anywhere. In order to get this sleazy serial killer off the street and into a prison cell, we're going to need to catch him in the act."

As much as he wanted to grab the man and haul him in for some close-quarter interrogation, Gabriel knew Shayla was right. He opened the door on the driver's side and got out, ready to head toward the convenience store.

"I guess it looks like we're going to have a long night ahead of us," he said just before he began walking toward the end of the block.

Chapter 24

Gabriel could feel an ache setting into his shoulders and his back. He rotated his shoulders, attempting to stretch a little in the limited space in the front seat. He glanced toward Shayla.

"Why don't you get into the back and stretch out there for a couple of hours?" Gabriel suggested.

They had been sitting out here, parked down the block from where their suspect lived, for hours. There had been no activity of any sort for a while now. An hour earlier, they had heard the unnerving sound of an approaching ambulance, but the emergency vehicle had continued on its way, and the distinct sounds eventually faded into the background.

Since then, there had been nothing except for the occasional vehicle passing by.

"That's okay," Shayla replied. "I'm fine right here."

Gabriel had different take on the situation. "Your eyelids are drooping," he pointed out.

"They're not drooping, I'm just blinking hard," Shayla countered stubbornly.

"Whatever," he said dismissively. "The point is that there's no need for both of us to lose sleep over this character. I'll stand watch and wake you up if I think there's anything going on."

"I can stand watch and wake you up just as easily," she replied.

It was dark inside the vehicle, but she just knew he was rolling his eyes. "Why is everything an argument with you?" Gabriel asked wearily.

"I am not arguing," she contradicted. "I'm just stating a counterpoint."

Gabriel sighed as he shook his head. This was futile and he knew it, so he just dropped the subject.

"For all we know," he told her, "the most likely suspect might not even go out tonight."

A movement down the block caught her eye, and she immediately sat up straight in the passenger seat. When she looked in his direction, Gabriel looked as if he was about to doze off himself. She reached for his forearm and shook it.

"What?" he asked Shayla.

"I think that's his car." Her eyes were glued to the silver BMW pulling out of the underground parking garage. "What time did Christine say Howard's night shift started?"

"Two a.m.," he answered, watching the same vehicle.

Shayla glanced at her watch. "It's eleven thirty," she said. "Kind of early for our pharmacist to be leaving for his shift, wouldn't you say?"

Gabriel was in total agreement. "It is. Let's see where this guy is going," he said. He started up his car but continued to keep it in Park. Watching the other vehicle intently, he mentally gave it to the count of fifteen before he finally started to follow the suspect.

Shayla could feel her entire body growing tense as she never took her eyes off the silver BMW. She knew that they couldn't follow it too closely or they might tip their hand. But on the other hand, they couldn't allow the vehicle to get too far ahead of them or they could lose track of it.

All things considered, this could all be a wild goose chase and she knew it, but somehow, Shayla didn't think so. There were just too many things pointing to the fact that this was their guy, however he might deign to arrange the order of his name.

Gabriel began to consider the possible places that the killer might choose to go, hunting for his next victim.

"What's open this time of night around here?" he asked Shayla.

She thought for a moment. "Not much. Some all-night pharmacies, a few bars, a couple of convenience stores. The restaurants in the area are either already closed or are closing down."

The We're Open sign in front of a Tex-Mex restaurant went out just as she said that.

Shayla suddenly leaned forward, squinting a little as she tried to focus. She almost grabbed Gabriel's arm again. "Wait, I think our guy just circled back around the Tex-Mex restaurant and went down the back alley behind it." Shayla bit her lower lip, examining possibilities. "He could have a girlfriend working here and he's picking her up after she closes the place down."

Gabriel appeared rather dubious, even though he nodded. "I suppose he could."

"Or," she amended, her eyes sweeping over the almost-empty parking lot—there was only one vehicle there, an old, two-door car that had seen better days—"this could be his next victim."

She looked at Gabriel. He hadn't answered her. Instead, as he drove up slowly, he was intently staring at the area behind the restaurant. A silver vehicle was parked some distance away to the far side.

"That's his car," Gabriel said, his voice barely audible. There was no sign of the pharmacist. "My guess is that he must have slipped in the back."

This was it, Shayla thought. This was the crime scene they needed to make their arrest. She could *feel* it.

"Let's go," she urged Gabriel.

"It takes him a while to tie up his victims," her partner reminded her.

"All we need to do it catch him in the act of tying the woman up. And if Howard has that syringe in his possession…" Shayla's voice trailed off.

He knew what she was getting at, and it was all the urging he needed. Gabriel was out of the car like a shot.

Reaching the back door, he pulled at it to open it, but it wouldn't budge.

Stunned, he looked at Shayla. "He must have locked it."

One of the things her mother had taught her was to always be prepared for unexpected eventualities. This was one of them.

"Move over," she told Gabriel as she fished something out of her back pocket.

Gabriel stared at the long, thin metal object in her hand.

"What is that?" he asked. At first glance it looked to him like some sort of unorthodox skeleton key— but not quite.

She moved slightly so that her body blocked his view. "Something you never saw," she told Gabriel.

Inserting the thin, rodlike item into the lock, she angled it into position until it finally made a clicking sound.

Triumphant, she looked at her partner. "Push it."

He did, and at first the door stubbornly remained where it was. But on the second attempt, the door finally opened and moved.

Weapons drawn, Gabriel and Shayla made their way into the rear of the restaurant. They carefully walked through the darkened kitchen until they reached the edge of the actual serving area.

Howard was there, elaborately tying up his latest victim. Sensing their presence, he looked up and then bolted. He left his paralyzed victim half tied up and partially suspended from a low-hanging beam.

"Get her down!" Shayla cried to Gabriel as she ran after the serial killer. "If I try to do it, I might accidentally wind up strangling her." She knew that Gabriel was strong enough to hold the woman up as he cut away all the ties that surrounded her.

Caught in the act, Howard was running through the restaurant toward the exit, his one goal to get into his silver BMW and get away. Shayla kept pace, increasing her stride until she was almost able to catch up to him, silently blessing all those times she had gone running for exercise.

Suddenly, just as he reached the exit, the man she was chasing spun around to face her. At that moment, she realized that he was still holding the syringe in his hand.

Had he emptied the contents into his victim, or was there something left in the syringe?

The next moment, Howard was lunging toward her, the hand holding the syringe raised up high, ready to drive into her. The man was apparently banking on the idea that there was still something left in the syringe to inject.

Holding her weapon with both hands in order to steady her aim, Shayla cried out, "Stop where you are. I can't miss at this range."

"You're bluffing. You're not going to shoot me," Howard jeered, ready to drive the syringe into her.

"But I am!" Gabriel cried, materializing almost out of nowhere.

Pushing Shayla behind him, her partner got off two

shots. Each shot hit the Moonlight Killer in one of his knees.

Shrieking, the man went down, his body hitting the floor like a dropped bowling ball. The syringe he was all set to drive into Shayla fell from his hand.

Relieved, Shayla all but sagged against Gabriel. His arms quickly went around his partner to steady her.

Her heart was pounding so hard, she had trouble pulling herself together for a moment. Her first thoughts immediately focused on the intended victim's condition.

"Is the woman he was tying up alive?" she asked.

"I cut her out of that lethal spider's web he had spun around her," Gabriel told her, contemptuously looking down at the shrieking serial killer writhing on the floor. "This maniac injected her with that same drug he used on the other women. Fortunately, it's not a lethal dosage, so she should be able to come around within a few hours. They'll be able to give her something at the hospital to help counteract the effects more quickly."

Shayla couldn't begin to describe the relief she felt flooding through her. "Thank heavens for that," she said. It would have been absolutely awful if the woman had become the Moonlight Killer's latest victim.

"You tried to kill me!" Howard accused, rage emanating out of his every pore as he lay there, still bleeding.

Gabriel looked down at the Moonlight Killer. There was pure hatred in his eyes. "If I had wanted to kill you, you worthless piece of scum, you would have been dead by now," he said. "But you're not worth my going to prison for." He looked at Shayla, his tone changing as concern slipped in. "Are you sure you're all right?"

"I am terrific," she assured him with enthusiasm, her smile wide. Taking out her cell phone, she pressed a series of numbers on the keypad.

The moment she heard the other end being picked up, she stated her name and badge number, told the dispatch agent the nature of the crime that had been foiled, then requested that an ambulance be sent out.

Hanging up, she looked at Gabriel. "It's over," she said, hardly believing the words she was uttering. This had been such a nightmare. "It's actually over." Shayla looked back at the shrieking man on the floor with nothing but sheer contempt. "This slimeball's reign of terror is finally over."

"But not before he killed all those women," Gabriel said, his voice hollow.

She knew that Gabriel had to be thinking of his wife. Her heart ached for him. There was nothing she could do to change what had happened and she knew it, but she could try to get him to refocus his thoughts and look at the events that had happened now in a positive light.

"Think of it this way, Gabriel—you stopped this maniac from killing a lot more women. Because of what you and I just did, there is an entire legion of women who owe their lives to you, even if they don't realize it," she told her partner.

He wanted to see it her way, but it wasn't easy. "You do have a way of exaggerating."

She shook her head. "Not this time."

"Hey," Howard called out angrily. He tried to get

up, but his knees just couldn't support him and he fell. "I'm bleeding here!"

In the background came the familiar sound of approaching sirens.

Shayla regarded Howard with sheer contempt. "Looks like help is on the way." Turning toward Gabriel, she said, "I'm going to go see how our almost victim is doing. Would you mind staying here with him?" She wouldn't put it past the killer to try to crawl away.

"I mind staying in the same universe as this piece of garbage, but go, see how she's doing. I tried to make her as comfortable as possible under the circumstances, although how comfortable could she be with all her systems paralyzed? However, all things considered, I have to admit that my mind was on you, not on Howard's victim."

She smiled at Gabriel. "To be continued," she told him. "For now, I'll be right back," she promised as the sirens grew louder.

Gabriel had laid the Moonlight killer's potential victim down, cutting away the ropes and ties that Howard had used in order to get her to bring about her own demise.

She was conscious but still unable to move. Her eyes were alert and followed Shayla as she moved closer to her.

"I know you probably don't think so right now," she told the young woman, "but you are a very lucky lady. All the other victims who caught this maniac's attention are dead, but we managed to get to you in time to save you."

Crouching down, thinking that the woman was struggling to try to talk, Shayla leaned in closely to the woman's face.

The woman's lips did not move, but a single tear did trickle from her left eye and slid down her cheek.

"It'll be all right," Shayla promised the young woman, moved by her plight and what she had gone through. "You're a survivor. You need to hold on to that. No matter what else is going on, you *are* a survivor."

The sirens had finally stopped blaring. That meant that the ambulance and, hopefully, the crime scene investigative team had arrived and could begin working the scene.

Shayla squeezed the young woman's hand and then rose to her feet. "I'm going to let the CSI unit in so they can get started," she told the young woman. "The EMTs will take you to the hospital. All this—" she swept her hand in a circle over the victim, indicating the paralytic agent that had been used "—will all wear off soon."

Returning to the area where she had left Gabriel, Shayla saw that her partner was exactly where she had left him. He hadn't taken a single step toward the serial killer he had shot.

Shayla had to admit that she was relieved. There had been a small part of her that had been worried he might have allowed his fury to come to the surface.

Rejoining Gabriel, she only had enough time to tell him, "I think she's going to be all right," before the first responders began arriving.

Gabriel nodded. "She's in a lot better shape than

she would have been if we had gotten here ten minutes later," he agreed.

The next moment, the darkened restaurant came alive with police personnel: ambulance attendants and the CSI team, as well as several uniformed police officers, a couple of homicide detectives who had recently been assigned to the task force and Lieutenant Hollandale, who was keen to learn all the pertinent details how two of his detectives had managed to catch a serial killer had terrorized Southern California.

Chapter 25

By the time they finished giving their statements to the lieutenant and were finally free to go home, it was approaching dawn.

With Hollandale's congratulations ringing in his ears, Gabriel drove Shayla to her house, then followed her in and promptly fell into bed beside her, too exhausted to do anything but hold her.

They did wake up a few hours later and, fueled by the excitement of bringing down the notorious Moonlight Killer, they made love with an extreme intensity, not once but twice before they were finally spent again as they lay in each other's arms, silent except for the sound of their breathing.

Finally, Shayla turned toward her partner and, grasping at a sense of normalcy, she asked, "So, you're coming, right?"

Oddly enough, though the question came out of the blue, Gabriel knew exactly what she was referring to.

"Your uncle is still having that gathering?" he questioned.

She pulled up the sheet a little closer as she curled her body into his. "Oh, now more than ever," she told him. "Uncle Andrew doesn't need an actual reason to throw a party. This gives him one, and to his mind celebrating the successful capture of a cold-blooded serial killer is just about the best excuse for a party ever."

She could tell by the look on Gabriel's face that he was hoping to be able to wiggle out of going. "I have to tell you that once Uncle Andrew makes up his mind to have a party, nothing deters him. He once had a party right after an earthquake hit because, according to him, he had planned his first and the earthquake had only caused damage out in Death Valley, where no one lived." She smiled at Gabriel as she ran her hand along his cheek. "He's a very stubborn man."

"So, I have to come?" Gabriel asked, resigned that there didn't seem to be a way out without causing a great many problems.

"You have to come," she confirmed. "Besides, Uncle Andrew wants to celebrate the fact that you're a hero." She knew how the patriarch's mind worked. "You brought down the Moonlight Killer."

With the aura of lovemaking still tightly wrapped around him, Gabriel drew her closer to him and pressed a kiss to her forehead.

"It was a joint effort, Shayla," he reminded her.

"At the end, yes," she allowed. "But you were hunting him long before I ever joined forces with you." Her partner's determination was admirable. And then she laughed as she ruffled his hair, grateful that he wasn't giving her a hard time about going to the family gathering. "I promise you'll have a good time."

Gabriel smiled into her eyes. "I thought I just had a good time," he said, caressing her gently. He was utterly amazed at how much she had come to mean to him in such an incredibly short amount of time. If it wasn't physically impossible, he felt he could go on making love with her until he just expired.

"A *different* kind of good time," she said with a laugh.

In her heart, Shayla felt that Gabriel needed to be exposed to her family outside the parameters of work. He needed to discover firsthand what being around a family like hers meant. There was camaraderie, laughter and warmth involved, not to mention the bonding effect of being part of the family of law enforcement agents.

Turning her body farther into him, Shayla made her appeal. "Please? Do it for me."

The words took him by surprise, and he looked at her. "Are we at that point?" he asked her. "At a point when you can ask me to do something I wouldn't normally do because it's for you?"

The fact that they had gotten here without his even realizing it completely stunned him.

Shayla turned her face up to his, giving him no indication that her heart was pounding even harder now than it had been when she had faced down the serial killer.

"Aren't we?" she asked.

The ten seconds of silence that followed were possibly the longest ten seconds she could ever recall enduring.

And then he smiled at her. "I guess we are."

With a relieved laugh, Shayla sealed her mouth to his.

The next hour melted away as he made love with her all over again—for the first time.

At the last minute, as they stopped in front of Andrew Cavanaugh's large, welcoming two-story home, Gabriel drew Shayla aside and asked her seriously, "Do I genuflect before or after I enter?"

She hit his shoulder with the heel of her hand. "Neither. You smile and shake hands. Uncle Andrew will take care of the rest," she promised, then suggested, "Think of this as the first day of the rest of your life— if you so choose." She looked deeply into his eyes as she made the pronouncement.

Gabriel sighed. "You make it hard to say no," he told her as he rang the doorbell.

She winked at him. "I make it impossible to say no," she corrected playfully.

Whatever he might have said in response never materialized, because just then the front door swung open and Gabriel found himself looking up at a slightly older version of the chief of detectives, Andrew Cavanaugh, who had once been Aurora's chief of police.

At the moment, the still-handsome retired chief was

wearing a large navy blue apron, which, Gabriel caught himself thinking, that, strangely seemed to suit him…

The broad-shouldered family patriarch flashed a welcoming smile at the man standing beside Shayla. Clasping Gabriel's hand, Andrew shook it heartily.

"Andrew Cavanaugh," he said by way of a very unnecessary introduction. "Welcome to my home. It's not every day that I get to meet a hero for the first time."

The greeting left Gabriel momentarily speechless.

Andrew never missed a beat. Putting his arm around the younger man's shoulders, he drew Gabriel into his home, which was teeming with warm smells and even warmer conversation.

"Come in, come in," Andrew urged. "Meet the rest of the family." He glanced toward his niece. "Shayla can act as your tour guide. I'd do it myself, but I'm afraid that the quiche Lorraine is being temperamental at the moment and requires my attention," he explained. Gesturing around the interior of his house, he instructed, "Make yourself at home. Please." Then, turning toward his niece, the onetime chief of police said, "Shayla?"

It was enough.

She threaded her arm through Gabriel's and took over. "It'll be painless," she whispered into Gabriel's ear. Her eyes sparkled as she added, "There won't even be a quiz at the end of the evening."

The expression on Gabriel's face as she led him off to the next room said he had his doubts about how painless this experience was going to be.

But it turned out that he was wrong.

Shayla made the initial introductions, but then the

other members of her very extended family took over, wanting to learn firsthand the details regarding the capture of the cold-blooded serial killer who had trolled two counties and brought fear and death to what had turned out to be, at last count, a total of twenty young women.

Gabriel found himself sharing details he had forgotten he knew. In the process of doing that, he found that the dark aura that had haunted him for so long—intensified by Natalie's murder—began lessening until it reached the point that it no longer threatened to steal the very air he breathed.

"He looks like he's enjoying himself," Valri told her cousin as the computer tech joined Shayla.

Shayla smiled. The same thought had occurred to her as she watched her partner. She was thrilled to see Gabriel like this. The radiating anger and pain that had been the first things to strike her about the detective were no longer there, she thought.

Gabriel appeared younger somehow. And happier. It was an incredible improvement.

"Yes, he does," Shayla agreed. She turned toward her cousin. "Listen, I wanted to thank you again for everything that you did to get us moving in the right direction. We wouldn't have been able to do it without you."

Valri waved away her cousin's words. "No need to thank me. We're all part of one big team. That being said, I wouldn't say no to a steak sandwich from Malone's if it happened to appear on my desk," Valri said with a wink. And then she moved on to join another cluster of people.

Shayla smiled as she walked over toward her partner, who was, at the moment, talking to her brothers Ronan and Luke and her cousins Dugan and Bryce.

They were, of all things, comparing notes on serial killers.

This had all the signs of going on all night. Trying to prevent that, Shayla sneaked into the middle of the group.

"Sorry, guys, but I'm going to have to steal him away from you so he can get a breath of fresh air on the patio," she told the foursome gathered around her partner as she wove her arm through Gabriel's.

Ronan shook his head. "Trust our little sister to interrupt just when it was getting really interesting," he pretended to lament.

"Don't worry, I'll bring him back after we all get something to eat," she promised.

Gabriel didn't bother hiding his smile as soon as he had gotten a few feet away from the other men. "Were you coming to my rescue?" he asked, amused.

"Not your rescue, exactly," she answered, then admitted, "Much as I love them, my brothers and cousins have been known to be a little overwhelming at times."

"I didn't notice," Gabriel told her honestly. "This was the first time I was ever talking to a group of detectives when one or more wasn't trying to top me or each other. Your brothers and cousins seem like nice guys. I like them."

"You have no idea how happy I am to hear you say that. Not that I thought you could honestly say anything else," she told him in all sincerity. "They care about you, I can tell. As a matter of fact, my family is strongly invested in caring—about each other, about the community, about protecting those who can't protect themselves. However," she qualified, her eyes shining, "sometimes, it's nice to call a time-out and get a little space from them."

The afternoon air was cool and inviting as they stepped outside. Turning toward Gabriel, she smiled at him broadly. "I'm really glad you're here. In case you don't realize it, you have a standing invitation to come over any time you want."

"You mean for the next gathering?" he said, wanting to make sure that he understood.

"No, any time," she told him, then grinned. "It's like Uncle Andrew has this magic box in the kitchen. Any time anyone one comes over to the house, day or night, there's always something in the refrigerator to eat. Somehow, the man never seems to run out of food."

Amused as well as intrigued, Gabriel nodded. "I'll have to put that to the test sometime," he said.

Happily, Shayla immediately jumped on the obvious. "Does that mean you intend to keep coming over?"

He rolled that over in his head. "It might. As long as I keep getting invited."

"Consider this an open invitation," she told him.

Rather than dispute it or argue about the invitation, he surprised her by saying, in all seriousness, "I think I'd really like that."

Shayla found that her pulse was doing some really erratic things, especially when he slowly ran his hand along her back.

* * *

Although Gabriel couldn't wait to get her alone to-night, they wound up being two of the last people to leave. It was as if now that he had actually managed to stumble across a situation he had only believed ex-isted in storybooks meant for the very young, part of him was almost reluctant to leave. He was afraid that this was just a dream, or, like in the classic old musical *Brigadoon*, a place that only existed once every hun-dred years.

But finally, it was time to go.

He expressed his thanks to his host and hostess, not once but several times, and then with Shayla beside him, he left and drove his vehicle to her home.

"You were right," he told Shayla as he walked her to her door.

"I usually am," she answered, doing her best to keep a straight face. "But about what this time?"

"About your family. I really thought going there would be uncomfortable at best."

"And?" she coaxed.

"It wasn't," he said.

Shayla put her wrist to her forehead like an old-fashioned heroine. "Such effusion. I'm not sure I'm up to dealing with it."

"All right, wise guy," Gabriel conceded. "It was great."

"So the next time you're invited…?" She looked at him, letting her voice trail off.

He surrendered. "I'll come."

"Good," she declared. "Because you're invited for next week. I'll go into the details later."

He didn't understand. "Why aren't you going into them now?"

"Because now," she said, slowly unbuttoning her blouse, which, in his opinion, had many too many tiny buttons running up the front of it, "I have something better to do."

He began to watch her intently. "You have my full attention."

"Not tired of me yet?" she teased.

"Maybe—in a hundred years or so. But definitely not yet," he said just before he drew her into his arms and kissed her, long and hard, stealing her very breath away.

Kissed the woman who had miraculously remained with him despite his surly countenance and turned out to be his salvation, now and forever.

* * * * *

One night of passion with Marcus Jones led to a pregnancy Chloe Ryder didn't expect. And when a serial killer they captured launches a plan for revenge, Chloe wonders if she'll survive long enough to tell Marcus about their child...

Read on for a sneak preview of
The Agent's Deadly Liaison,
the latest book in Jennifer D. Bokal's sweeping Wyoming Nights *miniseries!*

"You think this is a joke? I wonder how many pieces of you I can cut away before you stop laughing."

On the counter lay a scalpel. Darcy picked it up. The handle was still stained with Gretchen's lifeblood. Chloe went cold as she realized that she'd pushed too hard for information.

Knife in hand, Darcy slowly, slowly approached the bed. Chloe pressed her back into the pillow, trying in vain to get distance from the killer and the knife. It did no good. Darcy pressed Chloe's shackled hand onto the railing and drew the blade across her palm. The metal was cold against her skin. She tried to jerk her hand away, but it was no use.

Darcy drove the blade into Chloe's flesh.

The cut burned, and for a moment, her vision filled with red. Then a seam opened in her hand. Blood began to weep from the wound. She balled her hand into a fist as her palm throbbed, and anger flooded her veins.

Chloe might've been handcuffed to a bed, but that didn't mean that she couldn't fight back.

"Damn you straight to hell," she growled.

With her free hand, Chloe pushed Darcy's chin back. At the same moment, she lifted her feet, kicking the killer in the chest. Darcy stumbled back before tumbling to the ground. Had Chloe been free, she would have had the advantage.

But shackled to the bed? Chloe had done nothing more than enrage a dangerous person.

Standing, Darcy brushed a loose strand of hair from her face. She smiled, then scoffed before echoing Chloe's words. "Damn me to hell? Hell doesn't frighten me, Chloe. Nothing does—especially not you."

Don't miss
The Agent's Deadly Liaison *by Jennifer D. Bokal,*
available July 2022 wherever
Harlequin Romantic Suspense books and
ebooks are sold.

Harlequin.com

HRSEXP0522

Get 4 FREE REWARDS!

We'll send you 2 FREE Books plus 2 FREE Mystery Gifts.

FREE Value Over $20

Both the **Harlequin Intrigue®** and **Harlequin® Romantic Suspense** series feature compelling novels filled with heart-racing action-packed romance that will keep you on the edge of your seat.

Love Harlequin romance?

DISCOVER.

Be the first to find out about promotions, news and exclusive content!

f Facebook.com/HarlequinBooks

🐦 Twitter.com/HarlequinBooks

📷 Instagram.com/HarlequinBooks

📌 Pinterest.com/HarlequinBooks

You Tube YouTube.com/HarlequinBooks

ReaderService.com

EXPLORE.

Sign up for the Harlequin e-newsletter and download a free book from any series at **TryHarlequin.com**

CONNECT.

Join our Harlequin community to share your thoughts and connect with other romance readers!
Facebook.com/groups/HarlequinConnection

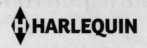
HARLEQUIN

Heartfelt or thrilling, passionate or uplifting—Harlequin is more than just happily-ever-after.

With twelve different series to choose from and new books available every month, you are sure to find stories that will move you, uplift you, inspire and delight you.